The Results of Not Counting the Costs

(Prisons Dilemma)

Chaplain Ken McCoy,
Doctor of Ministry

WESTBOW
P R E S S®
A DIVISION OF THOMAS NELSON
& ZONDERVAN

WestBow Press books may be ordered through booksellers or by contacting:

WestBow Press
A Division of Thomas Nelson & Zondervan
1663 Liberty Drive
Bloomington, IN 47403
www.westbowpress.com
1 (866) 928-1240

ISBN: 978-1-5127-1731-0 (sc)
ISBN: 978-1-5127-1732-7 (hc)
ISBN: 978-1-5127-1730-3 (e)

Library of Congress Control Number: 2015917473

Print information available on the last page.

WestBow Press rev. date: 10/20/2015

Contents

First and foremost, I humbly dedicate this book to the Trinity: Father God, my Lord and Savior Jesus Christ, and to my guide, teacher and comforter, the Holy Spirit of God. Your impact on my life has now defined everything I do. The price you have paid for me to have life and have it more abundantly is overwhelming. The only words I can say are "Thank You," because I can never repay You for what you have done for my family and me. All praise, glory and honor belong to You.

This book is also gratefully dedicated to the men and women who so selfishly give themselves every day to each of us in protecting society from those who can no longer live peacefully among us, whether the inmate's incarceration is for a season or for a lifetime. I'm speaking of the men and women of the Departments of Corrections across this great country. Whether they wear the badge, work in the medical departments, the counseling fields, work as support staff, administrative staff, whatever they do to cause us to feel safe, they are the unsung heroes of the law enforcement community. To you, I salute.

To those who have had to bury a loved one who died while serving the thousands of Corrections Departments across this county, I just want to say thank you for your loved one's service. You gave us a true friend: one who chose to lay down their lives for another. To you and your loved one, we are forever in your debt.

I know you may not always feel like someone cares about you, your service, or the standard in which you set; just know there are those like me who constantly keep you in prayer. If you don't already, you need to keep one another in your prayers. Just pray. Simply carry on a conversation with God.

There is nothing like working in a chosen career where you are seldom praised or even given credit for what you do. There is One who not only sees what you do, He also has a reward far greater than you can ever imagine.

Keep your head up and guard your heart and never let anyone convince you that you chose the wrong profession.

Be that example that changes the inmate's life. Good triumphs over evil every time. Ask God if you don't believe me.

Again, thank you from the depths of my heart for what you do for all of us. The greatest reward you will ever receive for the years of dedicated service to our citizens is, when you hear our Lord and Savior say to you, "Enter in, my good and faithful servant."

Dear Reader,

Content and subject matter are what's important about this book. The intentional use of incorrect subject pronouns is there to withhold numerous of the characters genders, ethnicities, and nationalities. I want you to be able to fill in those blanks.

I don't know if you have ever been arrested and had to spend the night in jail. I do know this; it can be one of the most life changing experiences ever. Having to do prison time is even more trying and unpredictable.

So, sit back, take you grammar hat off for the next hour or so, and hear what really happens when you get caught for not following your own good sense of what is right or wrong.

Whether you agree or not, man's laws are in place to protect us from the harm of others and ourselves. God's law was given to mankind to make each of us aware of sin. The law of God and the laws of man are similar in this fashion: neither could give life. It took the dying of our Lord Jesus Christ on the cross to accomplish that.

Praise God for His mercy and grace; and may the Lord enlighten you as you read.

Bless you always,
Dr. Ken McCoy

To

Every inmate: may you forevermore think before you act again, and may you learn to forgive yourself.

Every pre-teen and teenager: may you become the standard of what's right so that others will follow you instead of you following the wrong crowd.

Every college student: may you learn to set yourself apart from others so your choices will be your own.

Every parent and teacher: may you be just that. It's more important for you to be the adult than you to be a child's friend. Your guidance is what is needed.

Every person who has to be intoxicated to socialize and feel accepted: may you learn that you are okay just the way you were made. If you need a substance to please yourself or others, then please understand, there is a price to pay for your every choice.

May you find comfort in these words

Lamentations 3:22-23
It is of the Lord's mercies that we are not
consumed, because his compassions fail not.
They are new every morning: great is thy faithfulness.

Introduction

As the title suggest, there are consequences to not seeing in advance whether we are willing or able to pay the price for every action of our lives. We are accountable to someone, every one of us. This is a book that not only teaches you how to count financial costs; it opens up to you the other areas that need your attention as you evaluate your life choices.

It's a simple story about something millions of people do every day. For some reason, people think they can mix driving and intoxication together, and be okay. Our subject wasn't so lucky, if you believe in luck. They committed a crime while driving which cost them their freedom. They became a ward of the State prison system. Taxpayers footed their bill while they began to learn what they had done. They ended up with plenty of time to think.

It's a story of the stresses both on the incarcerated and their families, stressors on the workers in the prison system and on their families, the pain inflicted on the victims and their families, and on all of the law enforcement communities in general.

We will break down the many departments in a prison setting and a jail setting, and we will see the toll on both the workers and prisoners. We will even look at the families left behind, the prisoner's family that no longer has their loved one in their daily presence. We will look at the prison worker's family and see the burdens of not understanding why their loved ones do what they do for a living, especially when there are other careers out there less demanding with better pay and benefits.

We will learn what inmates need to learn to stay out of prison. We will see what the prison systems are actually teaching the incarcerated.

We will look at the demands put on the prison staff, the officers, and we will see if we can decide what puts so much stress on all the workers. Is it the demands put on by the departments themselves, or is it the undue pressure from the inmates?

We will take a look at some of the causes of incarceration. We will put blame, not condemnation, where it belongs when speaking of the incarcerated. We will try and draw a picture of the life choices that incarcerated men and women, and boys and girls, have now used to paint themselves into a corner. Their life choices, and that is what they are, will be examined and reviewed over and over again, so the costs of their actions can be put in physical, spiritual, and financial terms.

When we have finished looking at all the dilemmas caused by the incarceration of anyone, we will look for what brings hope in a thankless place and situation.

Chapter One

The simple arrest

Let's begin by seeing what happens the first time you are ever arrested. Let's look at the scene. Here you are getting pulled over by a police officer and you just had two drinks. The officer is walking up to your car and you try and put on your best face. You look into the mirror to make sure you look presentable, your eyes not to blood shot; and then your whole world changes. They want your licenses, so you hand them over. The officer walks back to their car. A few minutes later, they return. They notice you are nervous, and you feel as though you are about to wet yourself. (Just being real.) They tell you they noticed you were swerving, and ask, "Have you been drinking?" You admit you had, but you assure them you are okay to drive. They advise you to step out of the car, and of course, being confident you aren't impaired, you do so. You fail the sobriety test. You blow more than you ever thought possible. You even stumble when trying to walk a straight line. You find yourself being searched by the officer. You have handcuffs placed on you for the first time in your life. You don't think anything could be worse. You ask if you can make a quick phone call and the officer explains you can do that as soon as you get to the station. All of a sudden, it dawns on you that you are no longer in charge of this situation and you are rapidly losing all control.

At the station you have to be fingerprinted. You are told you can make a phone call in just a few minutes. You are so thankful when you are put in a holding cell. Now you can use the restroom, which you have had to do for the last thirty minutes. You relieve yourself, and then you notice you are not alone. Ten more people are in the same holding area with you, and they all just watched you use the toilet. You didn't even notice the cleanliness of the toilet. A quick glance and you see a month's worth of filth on it. You now realize that you might be more intoxicated than you thought before. Maybe you had more drinks than you thought. You reach to see your bar tab bill, but you don't have your wallet. How much more control can you lose?

After what seemed to be hours before finally getting to make a phone call, you see that it is three in the morning, and you have to call home so someone will come and bail you out of jail. The shame of it all hits you. You find yourself completely sober. Your spouse hears the phone announcement of the jail that an inmate is calling them; and you can hear them over the announcement, and they are crying uncontrollably. They accept the charges you have incurred on the phone bill. They are in a panic, because who knew if you were alive or dead? They certainly did not. You assure them you are okay, and you ask them if they will just please come get you out of here. You advise them to call the jail and see what it will take to get you out.

Unbeknownst to you, they are advised by the officer in charge that there is no bond for you at this time, and they are told you will have your first court appearance in the morning before a magistrate judge after nine o'clock. The jail personnel tells your spouse that they usually don't tell others this, but they advise them that you should make sure you have a good attorney, as you have some serious charges leveled against you.

By eight o'clock in the morning you are now boiling mad at your spouse. You think they just went back to sleep and forgot about you. You figure they are just teaching you a lesson.

What you don't know is they were up the rest of the night finding out what charges you are facing, and trying to find an attorney who would represent you. What you don't know is that someone called in on behalf of the person you accidentally side swiped and killed. That person, who is now lying in the morgue, was riding on their bike in the bike lane, and you never knew you hit them. But the fact remains, you did. Whether you ever remember the incident or not, you are now charged with someone else's death.

Thank God, for the dead person's family, someone saw you and they were cognizant enough to get your tag number and call the accident in. The arresting officer didn't even know this had happened. He just assumed he was pulling over a drunk driver.

You will never realize yourself what you have done to this other family. You will never have the capability of knowing how they feel. What was the value of that person's life to their family? You have robbed them forever of their loved one. There is no replacement for a life.

But you don't even know any of this yet. You are just waiting to give your spouse a real ear full. You are getting madder and madder at your spouse when you finally hear your name being called for court. Now you either hop a jail bus or walk down a long tunnel in order to finally arrive at court. You're still under the impression you are about to face a dui case. You are even counting the dollars, in your mind of course, which must be spent immediately to get you out of jail. You've got a number in your head. You're thinking a couple hundred dollars and all will be well, at least with the court system. You are still thinking what you are going to say to your spouse, but you know one thing for sure, you are going to give them a piece of your mind. You had to sit in that holding cell with all those criminals. What was your spouse thinking?

You enter court and see your spouse sitting with a stranger. That person is all dressed up, so you figure maybe your spouse thinks you need a good lawyer for your simple dui. You're still mad at them though. Leaving you in jail! What were they thinking?

Your name is called by the bailiff so you hop to your feet. It's time to go home, you think. The judge ask you if you understand the charges, and this strange fellow who has been sitting next to your spouse, stands and says he represents you and that he has not had time to explain the charges you face. You are still thinking, "What do you mean, it is just a simple dui."

So the judge asks you, "Would you like me to read the charges you face?" You answer yes, and then the bombshell falls. Your hearing goes bad when you hear hit and run, then dui resounds, but you were not ready when you heard the words, "Homicide by vehicle while dui."

You can now hear your spouse cry, and your head is spinning, so you don't know whether to cry or collapse. You hear the well-dressed fellow ask, "Is there a bond, your honor?" You hear the judge say, "I'll set a bond at $100,000, with the stipulation that your client give up their license. Is this stipulation okay with your client?" You hear your attorney say yes and you are immediately sent back to jail. There is absolutely no time to talk to your spouse.

As you arrive back at jail, you now find yourself in a dorm. More than fifty other people are there competing for bed space. There are only thirty beds in this dorm. You are suddenly gripped with a fear that you have never experienced before. You are not among the kind of people you usually associate with. You don't have a friend in the world with you.

"Welcome to your worst nightmare," someone hollers, and you begin to think it's true.

You realize it will take days for your spouse to raise enough money for the bail bondsman. You don't have that kind of money lying around the house. You start thinking important things now. What about your job? What about the rest of the family? What is your spouse going to tell them?

You ask if you can use the phone and the officers tell you what time they will be available. You count the minutes as you rehearse your story. Time drags before phones are finally available, and when your chance comes, no one answers. Panic hits again, and you know that sleep is out of the question. Your mattress is on the floor anyway; so how comfortable is that for you?

Reality is now setting in; you have actually been charged with taking someone else's life. Your life is totally disrupted by one simple act, and you can't even recall the incident. For the first time, you realize that your family's life has been thrown into turmoil. Nothing will ever be the same.

Somehow you slept, because you hear someone yell, "Chow call."

You look at what is served to you and think, "I can't eat that." It dawns on you that you haven't eaten since lunchtime yesterday. You take one bite and realize it is the worst food you have ever tasted. You feel helpless. You have no control of anything that is going on, and you have yet to speak to your family.

The morning passes ever so slowly. At noontime you hear your name called out for a visit. You are hoping it is your spouse, but it's your attorney. "What will happen now?" you say to yourself. You are about to find out. You have disrupted more lives than you have thought about because you have only been thinking of yourself. It's time to hear what your attorney has to say. All sorts of thoughts are now running through your head.

You finally arrive at the visitation area for attorneys. The officer removes the handcuffs and tells you to sit down and remain seated until your visit is over. You are now in the room with the person you had seen in the courtroom that had been sitting next to your spouse. They look different than you remember. You introduce yourself and they give you a business card. Life will never be the same as it was yesterday at this time. Your emotions are now out of control, for real.

Your attorney tells you that your spouse is okay, and that they plan to come and see you later in the day. They assure you the jail staff has said the visit will be approved. You breathe a small sigh of relief and you continue to listen.

What you are about to learn is the seriousness of your crime; yes, you are now a criminal in the eyes of the law. But you don't want to know what this means in terms of incarceration. You haven't even considered that yet. You are about to learn the financial costs to you and your family, or so you think. Your thinking is only on the price of getting out of jail. Reality won't set in until you speak with your spouse later on in the day. Your mind is still running a hundred miles an hour and you don't know how to stop it. All you are thinking about is gaining control of what's happening and getting out of this place. You can actually hear something inside of you yelling, "Help me."

The attorney hits the table you are sitting at and says to you, "Are you even listening to me?" You jump in your seat and settle back and put your eyes on him. You apologize and start to listen to what this man has to say. Fear of the unknown again grips you, but it is time to hear the facts of the case. For a moment, you are able to stop your mind from wandering.

Chapter Two

The visits

You study this guy's face as he speaks and you learn his name is Jason Brown. You know you have heard that name before. You recall that his face is on numerous billboards around the city. He is a 'dui' specialist. You even recall that years back he was a state prosecutor. You didn't vote for him back then, but maybe this guy can help. You start to listen more intently.

He says to you that your spouse has paid a retainer fee and that they are out right now talking with your family and their family about trying to raise enough money for your bail. He explains that it will take ten percent of the one hundred thousand dollar bail set by the court system to set you free while awaiting trial. He continues to talk, but your mind is set on thinking about the bail money. You are thinking about whom you could call besides your family to get such a sum. Maybe your boss, he likes you.

Your ears ring out again as he slaps the table. He shouts at you. "Can you not listen for just a few minutes? This won't take long, but you have got to listen!" You again focus on his face. He begins to tell you the facts. He now speaks with a slow, almost silent voice, so you will have to lean in and listen. "You are facing some serious time, at the minimum fifteen years. I think with your clean record, the prosecuting team will probably agree to fifteen years and let you serve seven of that in prison. I don't think you will find a better deal. And look, if you choose to try and fight this, you will probably receive a full twenty years to serve, especially if you want a jury trial."

You almost fall out of your seat. "These people want to give me time for this? You have got to be kidding," is your thought. He speaks to you again in that slow, almost silent voice. "You did cause the death of another human being. That human being was a son, husband, father, and a minister at one of the local churches. You have no idea what you have done to this family. Think about what I have said. This offer will probably be taken off the table by the prosecuting team within the next seventy-two hours. I'll be back tomorrow after you have talked with your spouse. I've already shared this information with them. Try to get some rest and I'll see you then."

He tells you he is off to see the prosecutor now. He stands up, goes over to the door and begins to knock loudly. Within just a few seconds, he is gone. Another door opens and you are escorted to the shakedown room. You are told to strip naked, and you think, what is this? You don't even remember being strip searched when you were first arrested. The officer explains to you that anytime you have a visit, go to medical or any other place in the jail besides your dorm, you will be strip searched.

All you can think of is getting out of this God forsaken place. You are escorted back to the dorm after shakedown and you notice all the inmates are staring at you. One shouts out, "Hey, your picture was just on TV. You ain't got a prayer." You just go to your mattress that is still on the floor and flop down on it. You want to cry so bad that it hurts, but something tells you not to. You are gripped by that fear you felt earlier. You feel eyes just staring at you. You don't know what you are going to do. You close your eyes and try to think yourself out of this place. You find that don't work, and you hear someone addressing you. You open your eyes and an older inmate's face is less than two inches from yours. You jump and they ask if they can sit down. You say yes and they say, "You look like you could use a drink." You laugh for the first time since your arrest. They laugh with you because they saw your story on the TV.

This person asks you if you remember anything about the incident. You say to them that the only thing you remember is being pulled over. They share with you that they are in jail for a similar charge and have been for several months. They say to you that they are going to fight the charges because the person they accidentally killed was also drunk and driving on the wrong side of the road. For once in your life that old saying, "Two wrongs don't make a right," makes sense to you. They share with you that their attorney tried to get them to accept a plea deal, but before they could accept it, the prosecutor took it off the table because of the toxicology report. You begin to think about what your report will say about your condition. They say to you one more thing and then get up and go to the other side of the dorm. Their words are piercing. They brought out emotions that you had literally forgotten you had. And yet, they were such simple words your grandmother said to you each time you got in trouble. "Have you thought about what you have done?" You wish you were back with your grandmother because you knew how she would always smooth things over for you. You put your face as deep into the mattress as you could and wept uncontrollably. You cried yourself to sleep trying not to think about what you had done. It was sleep that gave you little rest. You were still refusing to face reality. Somehow, someone else was to blame for all of this. You weren't a murderer. They have got this all wrong. This will be fixed. They will find the real criminal. "It's not me," you say, and so your thinking would just go on and on.

Grandmother's words soon escaped your thinking patterns. That stupid inmate didn't know anything about you or your problems. "Just forget about them," your mind said. Your mind went back to thinking about what you would say to your spouse. You rehearsed your words over and over. Lying words they were, but you kept rehearsing them. You couldn't stop yourself, and then you heard your name called again. It was visit time with the spouse. You quickly collected yourself and those thoughts turned into fear. What would this visit be like? You had no idea. Tears streamed down your face all the way to the visiting room. As you peered in through the glass you could see the same fear on your spouse's face. Your last thought before entering was, "God, what have I done?"

Before leaving the visitation room you will have that question answered, at least partially. You will know some of the pain you have caused your spouse and your kids. You will find out that your spouse's parents have written you off, once and for all. Your own parents will continue to pray for you, but your troubles are no longer theirs. Financial support stops at the attorney's fees. One of your worst fears ever has come to past; you no longer have a job. You have been fired.

You will recall over and over how that conversation went when you get back to your dorm. It is the last time you see or talk to your spouse for over a month. Oh, how you wish things were different.

As you go to where your spouse is sitting, you can't believe how many families are crowded into this little area. This is nothing like the room you and the attorney were in. There is absolutely no privacy. You can barely hear what your spouse is saying. You look for a better place to sit and finally spot one. You move to the corner of the room where there are two seats available. As you look at your spouse, you know they have not slept since you first called.

You start to talk and your spouse immediately cuts you off. "Look," they say. "You are going to listen to me for a change. I'm not in the mood to hear your excuses. You are out of control and all I have thought about is what the kids and I are going to do. The heartache you have caused our family is overwhelming, and neither my parents nor yours can take your substance abuse anymore!" You are dumbfounded. Your spouse has never talked to you that way before. "And another thing, the kids say they are never going to go back to their schools again. They can't face their friends and teachers because you are now the talk of the town. How many times have I told you not to drink and drive? And now this, all over the news; you killed somebody! Don't you understand?"

You're beside yourself. You feel like crawling out of the room, but that's not possible. "Do you have any idea who you killed? It was a preacher. You wouldn't know anything about that though; you haven't been to a church since we were married." Your spouse continues with their rant, but you have quit listening. Between the pity and shame you feel for yourself and the disdain you have for your spouse at this very minute, you just get up to leave. Your spouse says, "Wait," so you stop in your tracks. They ask you to sit down again and you do so.

They ask you to forgive them for the rant, and you say you will. They tell you about your boss calling and saying you no longer are welcomed back to the office. For a moment you think about the income you have just caused your family to lose. You look at your spouse and say, "Can you ever forgive me?" They say they will try but they also say it will be hard. They go ahead and tell you about the man you hit and killed. You learn that man had four kids and a wife that was going through her own struggles. You are overcome with grief and you confess to your spouse that you don't know what you are going to do.

You both share with one another about the conversations you have had with the attorney. Your spouse shares with you about the visit they had from the State Police. You learn more about your case. Not only was there one witness, there were several. One of them recognized you and your car. To the police it is an open and shut case.

You admit to your spouse that you cannot remember anything other than getting pulled over. You tell them you thought you only had two drinks, but you also confess that you can't be sure. You ask for the first time in your life, at least to your spouse, "What do you

11

think I should do?" They say for the family's sake you should accept the plea deal and not put any more financial burden on them. They assure you that in time, all the other things concerning the family can be worked out. They don't know how at this time, but they know they will manage. "Family will help out," they say.

Before leaving, your spouse says to you, "Somehow, you have to let the preacher's family know how sorry you are for what you have done. They might not be able to forgive you right now, but knowing they are people of God, they will come around."

That's the last words your spouse speaks to you for over a month. Somehow you know they are right. Your drinking and your attitude towards life have been your downfall. You again wish none of this happened, but it did.

After shakedown, you return to your dorm and look for the inmate you had talked with earlier. Maybe they can help you learn to cope with what has taken place in your life in the last day or so. You think for a minute and decide you can't even remember the date. You can't seem to find them so you go and sit in front of the TV and you find the news on. Surely they are done putting your story on. It only takes minutes before you see your face on the screen alongside of the minister that was killed. Instead of turning away in shame, you listen intently to the news anchor as he describes what a man the preacher was. You are stunned to learn that the preacher's wife only has months to live. She has stage four cancer, and unless a miracle comes her way, her young children will have to grow up without their natural parents. You can't believe any of this has happened. Right now you are so sick of yourself that you throw a dirty food tray across the room. Everybody in the dorm begins to scramble and someone yells for the officers. Within seconds, you find yourself on the floor, numerous officers on top of you, and cuffs and leg-irons being applied. Within less than a minute you are on the floor of a single cell. The door slams and you are told not to move. You hear radio traffic and an officer asking is everything

10-4? You hear someone say, "All clear." You realize they are talking about you.

After two hours someone says to you, "Can you behave now?" You look up from the floor and see two huge officers staring at you. You promise them you can, so they come into the cell and take their hardware off of you. They tell you not to get off the floor until the cell door closes. That's where you sleep until morning. You don't even get off the floor. That is where you find yourself for the next ten days, completely alone with your thoughts.

Still, you haven't done what your grandmother said.

After ten days you are placed back into one of the dormitories. During those ten days of segregation you had several visits from your attorney and learned he worked out a deal with the prosecutors. The only thing that could set the deal off is if the family of the deceased changes their minds. Their decision would be based on how they received you in the courtroom. If they saw you as unrepentant, then all deals were off. What did that even mean?

The next twenty days were the longest of your life, or so you thought. At five o'clock the next morning you were awakened by an officer yelling, "I said it is court time. Get your butt up, now!"

You hurry as fast as you can. You look through your stuff and pull out a piece of paper you have been writing on for weeks. You put it in your pocket and hurry along as the officer continues to yell. You reach the holding cell of the courthouse, and low and behold, you are strip searched. They take your little piece of paper away.

You find yourself empty of anything but your thoughts. You hope you can remember the words you wrote on that paper. Again, fear grips you. You sit and wait in anticipation.

Chapter Three

The trial- (plea time)

The holding cells are packed. A cell that was designed to hold ten inmates now holds more than twenty. Everyone is hot and irritable and it is extremely loud. You pray for the first time in years that you are making the right decision. Then the thought hits you; "Why would God even listen to me?"

An officer opens the door and calls out your name. You struggle to get out of the cell. You are thankful you only had to stay in there for just a few minutes. For the first time since you have been locked up, this officer speaks with kind words towards you. They tell you to be humble when you go before Judge Ivey; he can be tough. You thank them and think for just a moment, "Maybe God did hear me."

As you enter into the courtroom, you are told where to sit. You find that your case is the first on the docket for the day. You see your spouse and kids, and you begin to cry. The hurt that is on their faces is almost more than you can handle. You also see a young woman with four young children sitting right behind the prosecutor's table. Your heart begins to break. You look at her, and she smiles and cries at the same time. You just know this is the widow.

All you can do is stare and cry. You know you have no words that can fix this. You wish you could go over and express your heartfelt condolences, but you know you can't. The Judge speaks, and you slowly turn around towards him. He asks if both sides are ready. The prosecutor speaks and says, "Yes your Honor, we have reached a plea deal, if all parties agree to the terms." The Judge asks your attorney if this is true. He acknowledges that it is true. Both sets of attorneys are told to approach the bench.

They stand before the Judge's bench for at least ten minutes. You try and listen, but the Judge is speaking so softly, you can't make out one word of what is being said. Finally the attorneys return back to their seats. Judge Ivey speaks to you directly and says, "You will be sentenced as soon as Mrs. Thomas addresses the court and you. Do not get up or attempt to say anything. She does not want to hear your voice whatsoever today, and she especially doesn't want to hear any excuses. Do you understand?" You answer yes by nodding, and then for the first time in more years than you can count, you thank God. Since your little piece of paper was taken from you during the strip search, you had no idea what you would say. You actually feel a peace come over you. You know you would have not had the right words anyway; you just had one-liners on that piece of paper.

Mrs. Thomas stands up, motions for someone in the back of the courtroom to come forward, and that person escorts the children of the person you killed out of the room.

You can't help but weep, and you hear your spouse cry also. Your children are old enough to go out on their own, and that's what they do. Your spouse remains and just stares at Mrs. Thomas as she approaches the stand that has been provided for her to speak from. It is so quiet in the courtroom that you can hear your own pulse. Mrs. Thomas begins to speak.

"My name is Mary Thomas; I am twenty-eight years old. Those children are what God has given me so I can see my beloved husband every day in their faces. Even though he is no longer alive on this earth, I know he will live forever in their memories and mine. He was the best man I have ever known, other than Jesus. He cared so much for us, and he taught our kids the truth of life from the get-go. I'm here today so you can know what you have taken away from us.

He was someone's son; he was a father to the best kids ever, and as I said earlier, the best man I ever knew in the natural. He was my earthly husband, and he was a great provider. When I was down, he was always there to pick me up. Besides God, I was his number one. When I had given up my fight with cancer, he was there to push me forward. He would not let me give up, and now I know why. It is now up to God and me to raise these kids correctly. I believe with all my heart that if God can raise Jesus from the dead, then He can heal me from anything. I don't care what the doctors say; I will be around to see my grandchildren so I can tell them what a great man their grandfather was."

"Your taking his life away from me has given me more reason to live than ever before. I would give anything to have him back, but since that is not possible, the rest of my days will be spend raising my family and giving glory to God for what He has and will continue to do in our lives. You do not have the ability to rob me of my joy. Do you understand that?" You nodded yes; barely able to hold up your head due to all the shame you were feeling. She wasn't done yet.

"For a few moments after learning of his death, I wanted to chock the life out of whoever was responsible. I cried more than ever before. I could feel hate, which I had not felt since I had met this man, boiling up in me. But then I heard his voice. That voice which spoke from the pulpit every week. It was saying to me, "You have to love even your enemies." I thought about those words for days, over and over again. They wouldn't leave my heart or mind. Even days after the funeral, they disturbed my sleep.

Then an epiphany hit me. You, the person responsible for taking away the man I loved, were not an enemy. You weren't even someone we knew. You were just someone who made a terrible decision, which cost the life of another. No reason I could find in my heart was worth the hate that I wanted to hold on to. My husband's words, those he learned from God, set me free. My feelings toward you and your family are of sorrow and pity, not hate. The things you and your family will go through for the rest of your lives will be tougher than you can imagine. We have all lost something. I choose this day to not let one incident in my life define the rest of my years. I am here to tell you I forgive you, and I pray you can find forgiveness in your heart to forgive yourself. I also pray your spouse and children will learn to forgive you. Without forgiveness, we are nothing. You deserve another chance. That's the kind of God I serve.

Now, your sentencing today is based on one decision that you must make. I have talked with the prosecutors and they have shared it with the Judge. If you fail to agree with the decision I have made, then you can take your chance with a jury."

You hear her words, but you don't understand. You turn and look at your lawyer, but he just points you back to her. You feel fearful for just a moment, and then a peace overwhelms you. You question yourself because you don't know where this peace is coming from. And then she speaks again.

"The proposition is this. I want to be on your visitation list once you get to prison. I not only want you to see the growth of this man's children, I want you to see what only God can provide. I want you to see the forgiveness in me. And then there is one more thing; I want you to learn to count the costs of what you have done. I'm willing to teach you this if you are willing to put me on your list. It's up to you. You and your family are forever in my prayers."

She returns to her seat. Her children reenter the courtroom and sit next to their mom. She gives them all a hug. You notice your own children did not come back in. You look at your spouse and they have that smile on their face that you have been missing. You know what your answer will be when asked.

Judge Ivey calls the attorneys back to the bench. They are there less than a minute. They again return to their seats and your attorney writes a note to you. It says, "Do you agree to these terms?" You nod your head yes, and he approaches the Judge's beach. Now it is time to hear from the Judge. You listen intently as he addresses everyone there.

"In my lifetime, and I am an old man now, I have never witnessed such compassion as I witnessed today. I can't ever recall the time I cried while doing my job, but today I can't help it. Having lost a loved one in any situation is terrible, but having lost one because of someone else's poor decision-making is devastating. And then, to see this person's spouse stand up and forgive you is almost more than I can bear. I would love nothing more than to incarcerate you forever, but the law will not permit me to do that. If it were up to me this very minute, I would give you the full twenty years that is doable. Mrs. Thomas says, "No, this person deserves another chance." She also says she wants to help you. I truly don't understand, but I guess she sees something in you and your family that I can't see. All I see in front of me is a person who couldn't deal with life except with a drink in both hands. That is selfishness. It's pure foolishness. But I guess you are not the only person in life who thinks the answer is in the bottle. To me, all drunks are the same. You are all one mistake away from killing someone. I know; I see it almost every day. It is the one thing that has hardened my life towards folks like you."

You find yourself sweating profusely. You have never been talked to this way by anyone other than your spouse; and that only happened a few weeks back. You want to die at this very moment. You can't even remember the peace you felt just seconds ago. You fear hearing this man speak any more. And then he continues.

"Mrs. Thomas, I think you have changed this Judge's heart. I wish I could have your compassion. Maybe one day my lady, you can come and talk to me about God. I think I am ready to listen." You see the smile on Mrs. Thomas' face and you begin to weep uncontrollably. "How did she forgive me?" you think.

The Judge continues. "Will the defendant rise?" You stand with your head down. "Due to this woman's compassion, I sentence you to fifteen years, far less than what I want to, and instead of the seven years your attorney and the prosecutors agreed upon, Mrs. Thomas wants you to only serve five years in prison. Do you understand?" You nod yes. The Judge continues. "Mrs. Thomas, I hope you have made the right choice. Right now, I just don't see it. I pray you see the change that your God says can happen. Without good folks like you, this whole country would just go straight to hell. I mean that. Today, you have shown this old Judge what true love is. You have shown what God's grace is all about, and before you walked in the door, you would have never heard me talk about grace and love whatsoever. Thank you ma'am. I know your husband would be so proud. You make me want what you have. Please don't be a stranger to this court. I will be honest with you. Every defendant that walks in to this court today will benefit from your being here. Your compassion has just overwhelmed me. Thank you."

The Judge stood to his feet and walked away weeping. Mrs. Thomas had changed everyone's life in that courtroom. There was not one dry eye in the whole room.

Court was adjourned after that. Your attorney made special arrangements with the jail so he and your family could come and visit immediately. It was less than thirty minutes before you were ushered in to see them. You were so relieved for this entire trauma to be over with. You knew the right decision had been made. Even though you could not remember the accident, not even a glimpse of it, you knew you were responsible.

Chapter Four

Jail before prison

The visit with your family and your attorney went well. Mr. Brown was more surprised than you that Judge Ivey had accepted such a request for sentencing. He had never seen him do that before. He expressed his sincere hope that, after all of this was over, your family would be restored. He let your spouse and you know that if you ever needed him again, he was available. With that, he was gone.

Your spouse and kids put on their best face possible, knowing they would not be seeing you very much over the next several years. They assured you they would visit when possible and write when they could. Your spouse said their employer would give them as much work as possible to help make up for the financial loss of your income. It was tough listening to the hurt that was in each of them. You knew you had changed their lives for the worse. You told each of them you loved them and hoped one day they could forgive you. You assured your spouse you would try and not be a financial burden to them. They said they would do what they could, but not to expect much. Everyone hugged and tears flowed down each person's cheeks. With that, the visit was over.

After shakedown, you went back to the dorm, not knowing what you felt. You were glad the court case was over. You had seen more compassion that day than ever before. Still, something didn't seem right. You began to pray that you would wake up from this bad dream, and wake up you did. In fact, you didn't sleep for the next several days: not one wink. You could not stop thinking about what Mrs. Thomas had said about wanting to teach you how to count the costs of what you had done. Those words haunted you day and night. It got so bad that you finally signed up to go to medical. You needed sleep, so you explained your problem to the visiting doctor. He listened and explained that it was guilt haunting you. You didn't buy that, so you asked if there was some other theory. He smiled and said, "Yes, you are just looking for a way to get high. I'm not one who gives out drugs, so maybe you should see the psychologist to help you work through this." With that, you were sent back to the dorm without any medication.

Three more days without sleep, you finally went off the grid. Again you were segregated, and it was the best thing possible. You literally slept for ninety-six straight hours. The officers could not even wake you up. Medical staff would come and make sure you were breathing. They would check your vitals. And then finally, you woke up. You were refreshed. You wrote and told your spouse what had happened. You felt good and even the staff at the jail could tell you were better. You even thought to yourself, "If only I could have dealt with my problems like this while I was on the streets."

Your spouse showed up for a visit about a week later. The kids did not want to come because this place 'bummed' them out. Your spouse explained to you that the kids finally went back to their old schools and that everyone had been extra kind to them. They had found out that several of their classmates had parents who were either incarcerated or had been jailbirds more than once. The kids even explained to your spouse that one class they attended spent days talking about prison, and the effects it had on society. This was helping the kids adjust to their new life more than your spouse. Your spouse explained the hard times they were having making ends meet. They also expressed that they did not want to have to move in with their parents again. They said they might have to get a second job. The extra hours they were getting at their present job just weren't enough.

You could feel yourself getting depressed over this visit. All the troubles your spouse was having were due to your foolishness. You didn't have it in you to give them any hope. You wanted this visit to end, but you knew it shouldn't end like this. You asked if there was anything you could do to help them out. They just laughed. It broke the ice, and they apologized for getting you further down than what you already were. You shared with them what you had not been able to share with them for years, and that was the fact that you weren't very good at handling any kind of problem. You told them all you ever did was offer a drink to your problems. The next morning the problems were there again. You were able for the first time in your married life to be completely open with your spouse.

For the next hour you both talked about things you had never talked about before, about each other's feelings and the way you made each other feel. You were actually being honest with your spouse. You were behind bars, but this was the most you had felt free in years. Why had it taken such a tragic accident to bring you close together? You wish this conversation could last forever, but notice was announced over the intercom that visitation would be over in five minutes. You stood to your feet and told your spouse to go ahead and get out of here and beat the crowd. For the first time since the accident, your spouse kissed you on the cheek. You squeezed their hands tenderly, and your spouse left.

After you were back in the dorm, you began to think about how your mood changed from time to time. You had never allowed yourself to have such thoughts. You even thought about what Mrs. Thomas had said. You considered counting the costs of what you had done. That thought stopped as soon as you considered what you had done to your spouse's life. This thinking process wasn't fun anymore. The hurt was too much. Once again, you had put off the inevitable.

Days came and went without hearing or seeing your family. You began to worry. You hoped nothing was wrong. Saturday came and went without a visit. You felt depressed, but you knew it did you no good to worry. You fell asleep after Sunday morning breakfast and awoke to hear you had a visit. You were elated to see your spouse and kids; and for once, the kids were happy to see you. They told you all about the classes they had attended that were helping them cope with their new lives. They told you about families you had known for years that had loved ones in prison, and you never had a clue. They made new friends almost every day because of similar tragedies. Your son even shared with you that he was taking a part time job at a local grocery store to help out with the family finances. You told him you were very proud.

Your spouse shared with you some of the things going on with their job. Their employer had given them a raise due to their good work. They let you know they would not be taking on an extra job. You were relieved to hear that.

You let them know of your good news. Your court papers had been sent to the Corrections Department and you should be entering prison within just a few weeks. Your attorney had come by and shared that information with you. You shared with them that you had no idea where you would be sent, but you assured them it had to be better than this place. The visit was over way too soon for you, but your family was having dinner with your parents so they had to get on the road. You said your good byes, shared hugs, and that was the last time you saw them before entering the prison system. Somehow, they just weren't able to visit before you were sent to the big house.

As for the weeks before you left the jail, the climate there changed for the worse. Two people had been stabbed in your dorm. Violence had broken out all over the place. You feared going to sleep every night. Most everyone in the jail knew someone there. You didn't have anyone to watch your back. Fear was your own worst enemy for several days, and again you found yourself unable to cope. You wrote medical so someone could direct you towards help. Of all people to send you to, they arranged for you to see the Chaplain. After seeing them, they contacted security staff and you were segregated voluntarily until you left for prison.

You thought nothing could be worse than jail, but were you ever wrong. You were on the prison bus traveling on roads you never knew existed. You didn't even know your State had swamps, but there they were. You had no idea where you were. You didn't know what direction the bus was traveling in. All you knew right now was how much you would like having these belly chains and leg-irons off.

The inmate sitting next to you tried to get you to open up to them. You explained to them that you weren't in the mood to talk, so for the next three hours all you did was think. And think you did. You thought about family, about your old co-workers, about the people you liked to drink with, and your mind starting running over things that had not even happened yet. And then you started to think about jail. You asked yourself questions that you were actually able to figure out.

You first thought about the arresting officer. You thought about why they were so cold to you. It took you less than a minute to put yourself in their place. Imagine, you thought, having to pull someone over that you did not know. Would that person be cooperative? Would they pull a weapon on you? Would they want to fight just for the sport of it? You scared yourself. You knew you could never work a job like that. Then you thought about the intake officers. They had to deal with everybody being arrested, no matter what the crime was. They fingerprinted everybody, strip searched everyone, and all you could think about was how nasty their job was. You didn't remember much about intake, but you knew you could never ever work such a job. You thought it was as dangerous as the street officer's job.

Your thoughts turned towards the dormitory officers. What a sick place jail was. How could anyone work in such an environment? They received no respect from the inmates. They were cussed out, spit upon, and they fought almost every day with some fool. And their supervisors weren't treated any better. You began to question why anyone would become an officer at all. Then the thought hit you. You would never be able to do such a job anyway, because you were now a felon. You would always be looked at as a criminal for now on. Your life was an open book now.

Your thinking went back to those positions in the jail world. Your experience with the medical staff had been a disaster. They were even colder than the officers. They would hardly budge for anyone. You remembered them not even giving you something for sleep. You remembered that doctor saying to you that you were only there to get something to get high on. You resented that remark. What you could not remember was, being checked out by them when you first entered the jail. You were too drunk to remember that you threatened all of them. You did think about how many inmates were in the jail and how many different stories the medical staff probably heard daily. You knew every inmate there wanted something prescribed to him or her so they could just cope. Nope, you didn't want that job either.

The other medical specialists the jail contracted with were probably sharper than all the others combined. None of them would budge when it came to writing prescriptions. If you needed something that serious, then they would just transfer you to the hospital. They were not going to jeopardize their licenses for an inmate. You decided you wouldn't want their job either.

That only left one position that you hadn't thought about, and that was the sheriff. Too much responsibility, you thought. So you closed the book on jail. You really hadn't done to well there. You hoped prison life would be different. Maybe it would be a more upbeat place. Then you thought, "I really don't know what to expect." You had never known anyone personal that had done time. Not one person on your side of the family had ever done time. Your spouse had never mentioned anything about anyone in their family being incarcerated. You were at a loss.

One thing about time though, it just keeps going.

Then the thought hit you. You had not even given one ounce of thought to the jail Chaplain. You didn't even consider their position of employment as a part of the staff at the jail. But then it occurred to you that the Chaplain was the only person who had really listened and offered a solution to your problems. Then you thought again, "I could never handle a job like that. I don't even know what I believe."

Within ten minutes of your last thought, the bus turned on to this long driveway full of cracks and divots. What an old road, you thought. It must be fifty years old. You were close; it was sixty years old and only paved one time.

As the bus meandered down the long drive, you could see the prison sign on the front lawn. In huge letters was written these words: "State Prison and Diagnostic Center, established for the safety of the public." How weird, you thought.

You could hear inmates yelling out of the windows of the prison. "Fresh meat everybody!" You had no idea what that meant. Once again, fear had crept in.

Chapter Five

The diagnostic center

You thought jail intake was bad. It was heaven compared to prison intake. You and your bus mates waddled into the intake room. It had taken you almost ten minutes just to walk from the bus into intake, and it was only a hundred yards away. Once all fifty inmates had their belly chains and leg-irons removed, all of you were told to strip naked. It's the first time since high school you had been naked with anyone other than your spouse, well, except for the jail personnel. There were fifty of you in one small area. You were afraid to turn around, in fear you would touch some other naked person. You were told to bend over and spread your cheeks. You almost threw up at the stench. You had never been deloused in your life. But here you were with fifty others, being sprayed down. Your head was shaved, as no lice are permitted in prison. Male and female prison intake works the same as far as hair goes, at least in the State you resided in. You were marched through the shower like a bunch of cattle. Anytime any inmate spoke out of turn, officers pounced on that person with an array of cuss words you had never heard of. You stood in line naked while clothes were thrown at you. The last things you received from the intake officers were your shoes and a net bag to put all of the gear you had just been given in to. The whole intake process took less than ten minutes.

You were marched, yes marched, to the medical area where you stripped again to see if you had any visual defects, including sores on your body. You received shots for things you had never heard of. You were checked for tuberculosis. Your mouth was looked at. All sorts of medical cards were created and put in a file with your name and prison number on the outside of it. Again, the process was so quick that you had no time to ask any questions. By the end of the first day, you were worn out. You looked forward to having dinner and going to bed. Well, not so much the dinner. It was almost as bad as the jail's food was.

As soon as chow was over, you and all of your bus mates were escorted into the gymnasium. You were issued mattresses, sheets, pillows and pillowcases. Dorm numbers and cell numbers were called out for each individual, and again, it was off to the races. When you reached your dorm, that fear you had been battling for the last few months, was there to greet you again. You were awestruck at the size of the place. There were over one hundred cells in this one dorm, and it was three stories high. When you looked at the size of your cellmate, you felt they were just as big as the dorm. They took the bottom bunk without saying a word to you. You wanted to use the toilet, but all of a sudden your body rejected the idea, because you didn't want to drop your clothes in front of this person. You were as scared as you had ever been. You climbed onto the top bunk and you immediately played like you were asleep. You and your cellmate didn't speak until morning. You got up first, so you could use the toilet and sink without the threat of being watched by this huge creature. You were thankful they did not get up until the morning count began.

That was something different. There were more counts in a prison then there were days in a week. You found that strange, but you soon learned it had a purpose.

Diagnostics was the most fast paced place you had ever been in your life. Chow was fast and quiet. No one could speak but the officers. You were rushed in and rushed out. If the food had a taste, you really didn't know it. Salt was the only spice and it wasn't in great quantity. You sure missed those meals at home with the family.

Testing of all sorts would be the norm for the next several days. What took weeks before was only taking days in diagnostics now. And that cellmate of yours, they turned out to be pretty good people. They taught you the ropes of the prison system. They were beginning their fourth incarceration. They had the same problem you had; they loved to drink. They would be in prison for a longer stint than ever before. They had shot their spouse this time during a drunken rage. You had something in common, as neither of you could remember the incident in which you were incarcerated for.

The things they taught you about prison life would be invaluable. They taught you survival skills, and they made sure you knew that everyone in prison had a special skill. You would just have to find yours. They even helped you find it by asking you what you did on the street for a living. You shared with them that you sold pharmaceuticals for a living. They assured you that you could make a good living in prison. All you would have to do is identify pills that other inmates came across.

They also let you know that snitches in prison didn't last very long. Neither did folks who thought they could make it on their own. Someone had to watch your back for you.

With the information you had received from this person, you thought maybe you could make it.

All in all, diagnostics wasn't as bad as you had thought. Oh, again you had seen a stabbing, numerous fights, officers literally dragging inmates off to the hole, prison talk for segregation and isolation, but you had yet to see a killing. Gangs didn't rear their heads during diagnostics. Too many officers worked at this place to put up with any gang activity or attitude, but you would find out later on at other prisons that gangs ran all sorts of criminal activities. You would also find out along the way, that your diagnostic cellmate would be killed in a prison gangbang. You would find out that they refused to join a certain gang and was murdered right in front of officers.

Your last day of diagnostics proved tougher than you thought. As you were ready to board a bus to another prison, an inmate who you had never laid eyes on, cold-cocked you. The only thing you remember is waking up in the medical section of the prison. You received fifteen stitches across your left eye. Your only thought was, "How good will I look to my spouse now?"

The next transfer day, you and your prison clothes were loaded onto the bus heading south. What a thrill.

Chapter Six

Prison 101

If you thought you could be at another prison in your state any further from home, you were wrong. You found yourself only five miles from the State line. What that meant was you were three hundred and fifty miles from your family home. You know you received few visits from family when you were in jail, and that was only twenty minutes from the house. You had no way of knowing, but you would be at this prison for the next few years, and visits for you would be at a minimum.

You were not the only inmate in this predicament. Most inmates in this prison were from the north. Prison has a way of saying, welcome, and this is 'the usual' for most all prisoners. You think the system wants you to be as far from home as possible, but it just works out that way. Certain prisons have different missions than others. Even judging by length of sentence and by crime severity, you didn't think yours was so bad. The fact remained you had killed someone. What did that mean for you? You would live amongst murderers for some time. Was that fair?

Was it fair you had killed an innocent person? Not to his family. So where you ended up was because of your actions, not anyone else's. It would take you months to understand that, and the more you understood about prison life, the more you would find yourself alone. Your days would creep along, and your mistrust for people would grow by the day.

If prison were going to teach you anything, it would be the fact that there are few people in this world that really care about others. And you learned that you were no different. You saw inmates hated not only each other, but also, everyone else they came in contact with. You found this group of people was the most egocentric people ever. You could not stand being around folks that were just like you, and you didn't know you were like this, until you came to prison. What a sad life it had become.

What you did decide was you would start writing your spouse and kids after your first phone call to them. Your first call from this prison was paid for by the State. You got to make a phone call from the counselor's office the first day you got there. Your spouse answered and was very happy to hear from you. It did sadden them to hear you were so far away. They promised a visit the first month and assured you they would bring the kids. You promised no more calls, as other inmates had told you how costly it was to place a call from this place. Even illegal cell phone use was at a premium and you had nothing to barter with. Your spouse agreed they would write more often than they had while you were in jail. The call was pleasant, but it was also short; five minutes was the limit. You promised your spouse directions to the prison would be in the mail as soon as possible. You hung up and started to leave the office when the counselor told you to reseat yourself. You turned back around and sat down. They told you that this prison was very unique. They said it had not had an escape in the last forty years. You assured them you had no intentions of escaping. They said the telling you of the escape history of this prison was a part of the prison orientation, which they must complete with every inmate. You sat back and began to listen. You thought you had heard everything in the diagnostic center orientation, but they had only scratched the surface. What you learned from this counselor was this prison indeed was unique. They averaged two killings a month, the highest in the State, and third among all prisons in the country. Due to this stat, every time a killing occurred, no one could leave their cell for one week after such an incident, and sometimes longer. You learned all recreation calls were in your immediate dorm yard only, and that the gymnasium was closed permanently due to violence within the prison. You learned that every inmate would be assigned a job, no matter how menial. You were questioned about your educational level, your work history, family history, gang involvement, and goals after prison. You were able to talk about your crime and what it had done to your family and finances. Your counselor also advised you that a Mrs. Mary Thomas and her four children had been added to your visitation list per a court order. You were handed a blank visitation list and told to bring it back tomorrow when you were called back to the office. With that, you left for your new dorm with all of your belongings.

This was a huge prison, and you could not walk anywhere where there wasn't a fence within five feet of you; two fences surrounded every building inside this prison. As you were being escorted to your dorm, you noticed that you were the only inmate on the outside of any of the buildings. When you arrived at your building, the officer who escorted you called over the radio to get you entrance into that particular yard. He escorted you to the door, removed his cuffs from your hands, and left you with the dorm officer. Again, you looked around, and saw no inmates. The officer spoke up and advised you that everyone was locked down due to a killing still under investigation. He escorted you up to your cell and unlocked the door. You stepped in, and you didn't leave that room again for the next six days. The counselor came by the next day and picked up your visitation form. You would not see them again for the next three months.

It was a good thing you got along with your new roommate. Every one wasn't so lucky there. The last killing, you learned, was in your building and it was due to a squabble between roommates.

What you learned from your new cellmate was most people at this prison had at least fifteen or more years to serve. Some were serving life without parole sentences. They advised you that you would probably need to join a gang just for protections sake, or you might not survive. You let them know you were not interested, and they showed you scars to prove to you that it would be worth your time. You said you would consider it, but you didn't cause trouble and you thought that would probably be enough to satisfy most people. They laughed and said, "Do as you please. Those stitches over your eye, they look pretty new to me. Whoever hit you at your last prison made it look like they were just playing. Prisoners don't hit here; they stab, kick, or chock you to death. There's little in between."

Time truly dragged, and lock down caused numerous problems. There had been no visitation for the past five weeks before your arrival. You decided to write your spouse and let them know the issues at this prison. You told them in your letter to not even think about coming to see you for at least three months. Maybe things would be a little better by then. You also told them that since everything was on lockdown, no one could go to work. You explained to them you were bored out of your mind and so was every other inmate. Before you knew it, you had written a thirteen-page letter to your spouse. You knew you couldn't mail it until the officer came by. They would have to pick the letter up from you and check to make sure you were indigent before turning it into the mailroom, because you had no stamps. You hoped when your spouse got the letter, they would at least send you some stamps so you could continue to mail out letters.

You were so happy when lock down was finally over. For the first time since your arrival, you got to go and eat a meal at the chow hall. Your first thought that morning was, what a long walk to go and eat. Only one building at a time went to chow, so the process was rather lengthy. It took more than an hour and a half to feed population. That day you learned there were more than two thousand inmates assigned to this institution. You also learned jobs were scarce and really menial, not anything like you thought the counselor had said. You, along with five others in your dorm, were responsible for picking up trash in your yard. It was a yard that was only fifty feet by fifty feet. But that was your detail and it lasted eight hours a day. You also learned every one of the inmates on detail belonged to the same gang. They all shared with you how dangerous a place this was. They protected one another and all it would cost you was loyalty to them: nothing else. Well, maybe a tattoo or two.

Several weeks of pressure from these inmates costs you a fight on the yard during rec call, and you found you were not very good at fighting. Maybe you could have defended yourself if you had only had to fight one person, but three inmates from a rival gang cornered you, threw you to the ground and kicked you over and over again until you ended up in medical with several broken ribs. No other gangs got involved since you had not thought you needed protection.

Medical did the best they could to make you feel better, but within two hours you found yourself back in your dorm. Since you were unwilling to help security find your attackers, you found yourself alone. It would only take one more beating before you found yourself, not only wanting protection, but also wanting a weapon so you could settle a score. Your co-workers on detail were more than happy to oblige you after joining their gang. They found you a piece of metal and taught you how to make a shank that would cut the toughest of inmates. Word got out quick among the inmates in the dorm that you had joined one of the hate groups and you were now ready to settle a score. Revenge was all you could think about.

Security intelligence had also got word that new weapons were in the dorm that you resided in. The three inmates that had originally beaten you had apparently ratted to security that you intended to cut one of them.

Security teams entered your building by the dozen. Numerous weapons, cell phones and large quantities of drugs were found, but your weapon was apparently nowhere on the premises. Security supervisors took this threat serious enough to again lock the entire prison down for another week. Tensions grew among the gangs trying to establish their superiority. This was an ongoing ritual.

The first day lockdown ended, some of your gang members were charged with attempted murder. All three of the rival gang members that had originally attacked you were sent by helicopter to the nearest hospital for stab wounds. You found out that your new friends didn't believe in not protecting one another. They would expect you to do the same for the next several years that you were there; and that you did, for a while. You were involved in more than three stabbings, which were never resolved by prison investigators. Even the State Police could not solve these crimes. Maybe, you thought, they don't even care.

You had most staff members fooled. Few believed you were involved in gang activity; none believed you would stab someone. But that was the kind of person you had become. You lost your way. You had only one visit from your family since being at this prison. You had told them you never wanted them near this place again due to the violent nature this prison portrayed.

Then one day, out of the blue, you were called to visitation. You thought, maybe they came back anyway. It had been a long time since the last visit, and you never discussed prison life to them in your letters anymore. You just shared things that were related to family. You didn't dare want prison staff to know any of your doings. So as you prepared to see family, you put on your best face.

You entered the visitation area and searched for your family while checking in with the officer. You looked harder, but still didn't see any familiar face. You finally asked the officer where your visitors were. He pointed to a family sitting in the far corner of the room. You almost fell over. It was Mary Thomas and her four children, and none of them looked the same as the last time you had seen them in the courtroom. The kids had grown tremendously, and Mrs. Thomas was much older looking than you remembered.

As you approached them, you wondered if you would have even recognized them if you had ran into them on the street. Of course, you looked different too. You had several new scares, tattoos, and you had put on about twenty pounds.

You went over to them and introduced yourself. Mrs. Thomas introduced herself and the children. Each child told their age and the grade they were now in. Mrs. Thomas shared how tough it was to finally decide the time was right in coming to see you. So she asked you the question you knew was coming. "Have you learned to count the costs of your actions?" You admitted that since this terrible accident had happened, you had started the process several times but hadn't gotten very far. She said that over the next few months she would be visiting more since her and her kids were staying nearby with family for summer vacation. She assured you that by summer's end, you would understand how to count the costs of anything that was happening or had ever happened in your life.

For just a minute, you had forgotten about your new family, the gang, and were thinking about this family and your real family back at home. What she said to you next stunned you almost out of your socks.

She advised you that she had arranged with the Department of Corrections to come and teach classes involving victim impact. She had convinced the Commissioner of Corrections and several other dignitaries that it would be a good idea if the inmates heard from the families left behind. She told you that she would not embarrass you during these classes, but your case would be one of those discussed by her. She assured you no other inmate would know that she and her family were your victims. Reality again set in like it hadn't in months and months.

All you had been doing was trying to survive incarceration, and had not given any thought to such a thing as this happening in your life.

The more she talked and asked questions, the more you found that this was the first person in your life that you could not lie to. You realized that you had lied to everyone in your life, including yours parents, siblings, spouse and kids, co-workers, and everyone you had met in prison. Even all of your gang family was victims of your lies. Your thought was, "Why can't I lie to this person?"

Before you could open your mouth, she said, "Are you having trouble thinking of what you want to say to me? Whatever it is, just don't tell me one of your lies. You have lied to everyone your whole life including yourself. It is now time to quit."

With that, she told you it was time to get the kids out of here. She said the counselor would be getting in touch concerning the classes. She wished you a good day, told you to stay away from trouble, and then gave you a hug. As she was walking away, she turned back around and said, "Trust me; that was harder for me than you." With that, visitation was over.

As you were leaving the shakedown area, an officer said to you that you had a nice looking family. You told him it wasn't your family, just some folks you had recently met. You were escorted back to your dorm and upon entering, you felt as alone as ever before. Your thought was now on Mrs. Thomas and how you had taken away her husband, her best friend, forever. How lonely she must be.

You entered your cell and refused to come out until morning. Grief overtook you. What pain you had caused others in your life.

Before finally falling asleep, your thought was, "Can I ever forgive myself for the things I have done?"

Chapter Seven

Trying to cope

After awakening early, and before count, you asked the dorm officer if you could have a medical request form. You filled it out and gave it back to them as soon as possible. You wanted to convince medical staff that you were sick so you could just stay in for the next several days and not have to deal with anyone other than your cellmate. You were having trouble dealing with your emotions and you were just sick of yourself for the hurt you had caused others and yourself. You were even having trouble dealing with the very fact that the crimes you had committed while incarcerated would probably eventually be found out. You hated having to depend on your so-called gang members for survival. You truly didn't like any of these people, but they were watching your back.

For the next three days, the only place you went was to the shower. You refused all food, as you thought to yourself that this would convince medical folks that you were really sick. You knew the security staff would report that you weren't eating at all. Your cellmate even told you they thought about asking security to move them, because they didn't want what you had.

You finally looked in the mirror the fourth day. You did look bad. After the noon count, medical personnel were called down to check on your status. You had achieved your goal. They moved you to medical segregation for observation purposes. With this, you continued this scheme another four days. You knew if you could outlast them until day ten, you would probably be either sent to the hospital or at least to a new dorm where you didn't know anybody. Either way, you felt you would be the winner. You were tired of dealing with your gang family and thought that you being moved would be the best thing possible.

When day ten arrived, you were indeed moved to the medical dorm. You found there were only five inmates assigned to this unit. You were hooked up to IV bags within minutes, and for the next three days, that is all the nourishment you had.

On day four of your new assignment, you began to have solid foods. The medical staff patted themselves on the back for your complete recovery, and within twenty-four hours you found yourself in a brand new dorm. Your goal was accomplished.

It took more than three days to meet all of the inmates in this new setting, and you knew no one there. You decided once and for all, you would no longer depend on anyone having to watch your back. You were done with that type lifestyle, even if it meant losing your life.

You started doing a survey of your prison life. You made notes on a sheet of paper that only you would understand. 'M' was for manipulation. You broke that category down to officers, staff, medical personnel and even inmates. You did your best to cover every day you had been in prison. Just then it dawned on you. Tomorrow would be your thirteenth month of being in prison. Nothing you had achieved was positive about this experience. Could you survive another forty-seven months?

You put your mind back on your sheet of paper again. 'C' would be for cutting. You counted the number of inmates you had stabbed. 'S' would be for scuffling. How many fights had you now had? You then depressed yourself. 'V' was the only thing you could think of for representing visits you had received. That was the easiest of all. You had had only one from your spouse and one from Mrs. Thomas. How sad, you thought; my parents won't even visit me. You then decided to add family to your manipulation category. You couldn't complete it because there were so many times you had used each of them. You got so upset with this now so-called game that you destroyed the sheet of paper you were writing on. "What a waste," you thought.

You figured Mrs. Thomas' class would be something like this. You could only do so much before you gave up. You thought about how you would react in front of the other inmates when this class was being taught about you. You were the reason for the class. Why was she teaching it like this instead of just doing it during visitation? You just didn't understand. You were tired of thinking about all of the harm you had caused others, so you went downstairs to watch television. You realized almost everyone in the dorm was glued to the tube. Of course, it was baseball season. With that, you settled into the game and your mind went blank. You set there long after the game and hadn't had one thought. You got up, went to your cell, and slept until morning.

After chow, you were called to the counselor's office. They advised you there would be a new detail assignment for you. That new assignment was attending a victim impact class, which would run for five weeks. You said, "That's it? I don't have a regular detail?" They said that is all there is. Class would be once a week for two hours and you would have several assignments to complete. With that, you again wouldn't see your counselor for several months.

You went back to the dorm and wrote to your spouse and kids. You sent them each separate letters. You told them about Mrs. Thomas and her kids coming for a visit. You even shared with them about the class Mrs. Thomas would be teaching. You shared with each of them that the class was now considered your detail assignment. You thought for a minute, "Wow, this is the first time I have talked about prison life to them in months." You wondered if prison staff would be suspicious of your writings since you hadn't mentioned anything whatsoever about prison in at least six months in any other letter. That thought soon faded. You let all of them know you were okay, and if they were ready, you were up to them visiting when possible. With that, you closed.

In just a few minutes, you heard loud noises coming from the dorm dayroom. You stepped outside of your cell along with your cellmate to see a brawl going on. You couldn't tell if it were five or six inmates fighting. You looked at your roommate, turned around, and went back into your cell. They followed right behind. You told them you didn't want any involvement and that you were done with fighting. They agreed and pulled hard on the door so it would lock. Soon, both of you could hear security coming in the dorm. It took less than a minute for all to be quiet. You didn't give it another thought until security was at your cell door telling you to step out. You were told there had been a killing and that everyone was under suspicion. They made you and your roommate strip naked, took pictures of each of you from the waist up, and then went to the next cell to do the same. They were looking for any type scratches or cuts.

You knew you had done nothing wrong this time, but fear was something that you wouldn't be able to shake for days. You feared your tattoos would get you in trouble. Your cellmate didn't have any, so you feared even more.

Days past, and finally everyone could again leave their cells. On your way to breakfast that morning, an officer you had never seen questioned you concerning the incident. You told them you had already answered the investigator's questions. They advised you they didn't care about that, and that their interest was in your gang tattoos. You told them you didn't know what they were talking about. They smiled and said, "Oh I believed you do. Numerous of your homies have now been charged with murder from previous incidents. Same tattoos, same hometown. Are you saying that is just a coincident? I don't think so."

You went on about your business the rest of the day. When your cellmate came back from detail that day, they told you they had been questioned about how well they knew you. You tried to put this out of your mind, but you just couldn't.

You heard nothing about this again for several days, and then what you heard was disturbing. The death toll from that fight you had seen was now up to two. Still, you knew you were not involved and so did everyone else in your dorm. Even your dorm officer had said you were not involved. You knew there was even video of this incident, but for some reason that did not comfort you. Those words from that strange officer, who had spoken to you days before, continued to haunt you.

You began to inquire about who this person was. It didn't take long for security intelligence to find out you were nosing around about this incident. You were summoned to the security office by several people twice your size. You denied any knowledge of such a thing.

You were amazed at what happened next. They showed you a dvd recording of the entire incident. They honed in on the killing, and on the tattoo of one the murdered victims. It was a tattoo just like one of yours. Their question to you was why you had not defended your partner. You told them the truth; you didn't even know this inmate. They didn't believe you but they also had nothing to hold you on. Their next words horrified you. They let you know that as soon as the rest of the gang finds out about you not coming to another member's aide, you would be dealt with severely. That usually meant death. But they said, they were only speculating. With that, you were escorted back to the dorm. As you entered the dorm, you felt as though several inmates were watching you.

All was quiet for hours, and then several inmates entered your cell and surrounded you. They wanted to know why you hadn't helped your homies, so you tossed it right back at them and said, "Why didn't you?" It was like a standoff for several minutes. You finally convinced them that you had only arrived at this particular dorm days before; and you didn't know who was who. They all showed you their tattoos; and you found yourself again surrounded by those who counted on you for protection. You did question them as to why they had not come to their own member's aide, but they just ignored your question. One suggested that it wasn't your responsibility to question their integrity. You knew what that meant. This person had been killed by their own gang.

You knew these people weren't like the other members you had known. This was personal what they had done, and you didn't want anything to do with them. Again, you told yourself, "I'm done with this gang life. I don't care what anybody says."

Tomorrow had to be a better day.

Chapter Eight

Mrs. Thomas' classes

One day, not long after Mrs. Thomas and her kids visited with you, you notice both staff and officers running around like crazy. You had no idea what was going on; so, being the person you are, you asked one of the officers. They informed you it was none of your business, so you asked other staff members. Finally one shared with you that the Commissioner of Corrections, along with other dignitaries, was on their way down for a visit. You thought it was due to the prison's reputation for being so violent, so you just shrugged it off and went about your miserable way. You figured lockdown could occur at any moment, so you went and found a good book to read. You had not been in your cell for over five minutes when the CERT team, (Correctional Emergency Response Team), came and escorted you to the security office. They had you a fresh change of clothing, a new pair of boots, and some papers for you to sign. As you read the papers, you saw you were giving permission for your personal information to be given to the media, along with a prison identification picture. You asked why this was necessary. That's when you found out how big a deal this was.

You found out not only was the Commissioner of Corrections on their way, but so was the Governor and all his entourage. What you learned was that Mrs. Thomas was beginning her class today, and it had the backing of the States' political party. You were also learning just what a powerful man you had killed. This young preacher was the Governor's best friend's son.

For the next hour you were instructed on how you would act while these visitors were here. You asked to see your counselor, but you were told they were not at the prison today. You were also told that the Warden would be seeing you very shortly. You started thinking that this was not what you had signed up for. You thought this class would be simple, short to the point, and make you think about what you had done for the rest of your life. You were partly right.

When the Warden entered into the room, so did Mrs. Thomas. The Warden's words were directly to the point: any foolishness and you would be locked down until further notice. But, Mrs. Thomas' words were mostly apologetic. She explained to the Warden and you that when she asked to do this class, she did not expect that it would become a political arena. She simply wanted to teach selected prisoners how to count the costs of what they had done. It was her hope this would change their lives for the good.

The Warden laughed and said, "Good luck with that," in a very sarcastic way. Not another word was said until all the politicians arrived. When the Governor walked in, Mrs. Thomas immediately got up, said a few words to him, and sat. The Governor looked a little dumbfounded, called the Commissioner of Corrections over, whispered something in their ear, and they all re-boarded their helicopters and left. Not one person explained anything to the Warden, so he just went back to his office, awaiting the Commissioner's call; and within minutes, the Commissioner explained to the Warden that whatever Mrs. Thomas needed for her class, it was to be made available. With that, you learned who was in charge of Mrs. Thomas class, and it wasn't the Governor or the Warden. It was God.

So for the next five weeks the classes went off without a problem. There wasn't a killing in the prison; in fact, there wasn't even a fight during Mrs. Thomas' time there. The class students, fifty-five gang members, basically stopped all gang activity so this class could do its thing. And its thing was powerful. A thousand preachers could not have accomplished in a year what Mrs. Thomas accomplished in five weeks. She taught inmates how to count the costs of everything they have ever done or will do in life; and she used your life as the example of what not to do.

From day one, you gave her permission to let everyone know that you were the reason she was there. It just made the class easier; and it made it possible for her to tell the story the way it should be told. So, here is how it went.

Week one class was about what was lost by everyone involved, dollar wise. The simple bar tab bill, which you thought was for two drinks, turned out to be for six. Forty dollars was the tab; much higher than you had imagined. The figures kept climbing, and your spouse had kept most of this to themselves. The retainer fee for your attorney, which was paid by your spouse, was five thousand dollars. You thought that was outrageous until you heard what the rest of the attorney's fees were: thirty thousand dollars to get you a plea deal. Your only thought was, "What have I done to my family?" That fee was paid for by your parents. That's why they had not come to see you, as you had cost them a portion of their life savings, and you knew they were on a fixed income. So far, your tab was at a staggering thirty-five thousand and forty dollars.

"Oh, but wait," Mrs. Thomas said, "your car was also confiscated that night, and it was actually paid for. It was an older model Chevrolet, but it was worth over eight thousand dollars."

You had never gotten this far with your counting the costs, and it just continued. Mrs. Thomas now brought up the job that you had lost. "Here's a person," she explained, "that made sixty-two thousand a year selling pharmaceuticals. Their job would have continued if they had not been incarcerated, so here is five years times sixty-two thousand dollars, or a whopping three-hundred and ten thousand dollars. Are all of you getting this picture? For just a few drinks?"

You found yourself amazed. But she still wasn't finished. With your spouse's permission, Mrs. Thomas told more of the story that you did not know. "Within the last two months," she said, "your family has lost their home to foreclosure and had to move into the home of your spouse's parents. The equity in the home was valued at fifty thousand dollars. Is anyone keeping a tab?"

One of the other prisoners spoke from the back of the room. "That's four hundred and three thousand and forty dollars. That is some expensive booze." Everyone laughed but you and Mrs. Thomas. Within seconds the class went silent, and an apology came from the back of the room; "Sorry ma'am, and sorry for your loss."

Mrs. Thomas thanked the other inmate for the apology and said, "The dollar costs for this loss will continue forever. Oh yeah, there was court cost also, just a mere six hundred dollars; and probation fees for ten years after the prison sentence is completed."

The total was now four hundred six thousand and forty dollars. You were now at a complete loss for what to say or think. In dollars, you had devastated your family forever.

Now it was time to hear about Mrs. Thomas' family in terms of dollar costs. "My husband's funeral cost was twelve thousand dollars. His bicycle was destroyed: another one thousand. Salary lost totaled was fifty-five thousand a year, and he was only twenty-nine years old. He had another thirty-seven good years that he would have worked, and he loved his work. If he had never gotten a raise increase, that would still have been an income of two million and thirty five thousand dollars in his lifetime. In terms of money, that might not seem like much to some of you, but if it were just money we were dealing with here, I could handle it. This is about life, about plans that have been ruined by one selfish person's act. We will continue here next week. Oh yeah, what's the total up to?"

The same prisoner in the back shouted, "Both families' loses stand at two million four hundred forty one thousand and forty dollars."

"Thank you," said Mrs. Thomas, "see you next week."

With that, security escorted her out and all of the inmates were escorted to shakedown. Mrs. Thomas had told the class that, what was discussed in the class should remain there. Pretty much so, that was the way it went.

Once you were back at your cell, you began to write your spouse and repeat how sorry you were for all the heartache you had caused. You explained how Mrs. Thomas had shared with the class what your spouse had shared with her concerning the loss of the house to foreclosure. You tried your best to share words of comfort, but you knew in your heart that they could not console your spouse and kids. How hard you had made it for each of them. Then you thought, almost out loud, "What will the next class bring?"

With that, you finished your letter and sealed it. You began to wonder if your spouse would even read it.

The rest of the week dragged by, but you continued to think of other costs your accident had incurred. How would that next class be? Would you feel as rotten as when the first class had ended?

Week two class was all about what your family had suffered. It was about separation, about the unknown of what could or would happen, and about the dreams of the kids being crushed due to your incarceration. Neither of the kids could ever afford college, even with the help of both sides of grandparents. Your spouse just couldn't make ends meet, and they sure didn't want to discuss that with you.

What was clear to you right now was how much your spouse and Mrs. Thomas shared with each other about their lives. It was as though they had become best of friends. Your spouse said very little to you in letters anymore. Maybe this was payback, you thought, since you didn't talk about prison life anymore. What you learned was that family wasn't family at all; each member left behind had gone their own way. Your spouse was having to work more and more; your son was failing school and had lost his job, and your daughter, well, who knew where she was. You actually had no idea that any of this was going on. You sat there traumatized, wanting to escape this room, but knowing it was high time you faced the facts. You finally raised your hand and Mrs. Thomas asked, "Is this too much information for one day?" You shook your head yes and she ended the class.

She was escorted out; but the inmates were left there for almost thirty minutes, unattended. In that timeframe, not one word was spoken by anyone: just dead silence. You wished you were dead. What a failure you were. You had given up everything for a drink. How could you ever face your family again?

You were thankful when the officers finally came in and escorted everyone to shakedown. Again, not one word was said by any inmate. An officer finally spoke up and asked, "What's the matter, cat got your tongues?" Still, nothing. It seemed to you that every inmate was searching their own heart and looking at all the evil they had brought to others.

The rest of the week didn't change the mood around this group of inmates. It was the most silent the prison had been in years. Even the staff began to think something was about to happen because no one was speaking. Lockdown was implemented for two days due to fear, but that changed nothing; so administration lifted the lockdown and things seem to go back to normal, except that no one was still speaking.

As the new class time approached, you were thankful that this class was having such an impact. You had learned in two weeks what it would have taken your spouse months to tell you. You also learned something about yourself. You were learning to handle life without one thought of getting high. That was an accomplishment.

Mrs. Thomas looked as if she was spooked about something, so one of the other inmates asked her, "Ma'am, is everything alright?" She smiled, said thanks for asking, and began to teach like never before. She opened up about her life. She shared with the class about her battle with cancer, and how close she had been to death. She shared that she had only been given weeks to live according to the doctors, before her husband's death. Then she shared the story of the courtroom drama, how she had shared with the court and judge that she now had a reason to live, and that reason was so she could share with her grandchildren what a great man their grandfather was. Again, this class was almost too much to handle.

She also shared with the class just what a great guy her husband was. She talked about their wedding day, the day each child was born, their first church, and then spoke about what a proud person she was for having such a husband. You could hear prisoners getting chocked up. Mrs. Thomas looked around and said to each individual, "Do you really know what you have done in this life? Do you know what pain you have caused others? Did you know that I wanted to strangle my husband's killer? Did you know that if I had not forgiven them I would be dead today? Today's class is about forgiveness. Whatever you have done, I forgive you. Now go and see if you can forgive yourself. Oh, guess what, you can't do it without God. Next week's class is on God's forgiveness. See you then."

With those words, she gave a big smile and off she went. What all of us inmates had found, was that without knowing it, we had been churched three weeks in a row. What an amazing person. She lived what she and her husband had preached their short lives together. And now their ministry was up to her. She knew her calling and she knew how to fulfill it. What every inmate in this room had learned in a short time was how to count the costs of something else before it ever happened.

Your thought rested with these words, "Will I remember this next year at this time?"

Excitement seemed to fill the air at the prison. Inmates were speaking again, and that's when it hit you, there had not been a fight in the three weeks since Mrs. Thomas had been coming to the prison. You figured there had to be a correlation. You decided to speak to other inmates about the behavior inside the prison. Believe it or not, no one had seemed to notice but you. You then asked some of your classmates. All of them had noticed. You even asked one of them if the prison itself had picked out the members of this class. The two of you agreed that it was a possibility. You both laughed about this and went your separate ways.

When you got back to the dorm, it was mail call. You got a letter from your spouse, and it sure explained a lot about why they had not written. They were too embarrassed to share with you about losing the house and not being able to control the kids. Both shame and guilt had attacked them. With what you had learned from Mrs. Thomas, you were able to see that you were to blame for all of this and not your spouse. So you sat down and took the blame like you should and composed the best letter you had ever written in your life. For the first time in months, you opened up to your spouse.

A mere three weeks had changed your life drastically. "If only I had known what I know now," was your thought. You wrote all night long; and when morning came, you made certain your letter got mailed.

Week four class was approaching rapidly. You thought about what you would be taught, but then put your mind back on what you had already been taught. That was what was important. And then tomorrow came.

You found these words written on the chalkboard in the classroom. Mrs. Thomas was tapping the chalk where the words ended. You began to read them: Luke 14:28, "For which of you, intending to build a tower, sitteth not down first, and counteth the cost, whether he have sufficient to finish it?"

You thought to yourself and then spoke it out loud, "Wow, that should have been up on the board the whole class." With that, Mrs. Thomas responded, "It could have been, but it is more appropriate for today's class. Let's see if you get why this also relates to forgiveness."

As she explained what forgiveness really is, she also spoke to the fact that you have to live it; it's not just something you give once and that's it. Then she explained how she and her husband had taught it in the church for years, but all that teaching just seemed mere words now. What she said next would change your life forever. She said, "Before you can ever complete the task of counting the costs, you have to see if you have enough forgiveness in yourself to finish the complete job of forgiveness. You see, words are cheap; they mean nothing if you are not willing to lose everything and still have enough in you to forgive whomever has robbed you." With that, she looked right at you and said, "Remember the day we were in court and I said I forgave you? That wasn't me. Well, it was my spirit man, but it wasn't my whole being. Remember when I saw you in visitation and hugged you, that also was my spirit man, not my whole being. Look at me really well today. Today, my whole being forgives you. God showed me forgiveness; and He says to each of us that if we want forgiveness then we can only achieve it by forgiving others completely. Do you know what? He also said to me that my husband could have forgiven you completely the first day, not just in his spirit, but also, with his whole man, even if you had killed me and the kids instead of him. That is forgiveness. But it doesn't stop there. Did you know you were forgiven for every sin you ever committed when Jesus hung on that cross and died? He saw you while he was hanging there and he forgave you of everything evil you ever did or will do: past, present and future. That's why I can forgive; and I choose to forgive and I choose to never bring it up again to you, ever. It is finished."

With that she left the class with tears still running down her face. As you sat there, you could feel every eye in the room staring at you. You felt so low, but you also knew that this person had totally forgiven you of all the hurt you had caused them. You stood up and went to the front of the class and said, "This is the hardest thing I have ever gone through; but it is nothing compared to what this lady has suffered. How she can forgive and forget is beyond me, but this is the life I want. I want the ability to not only forgive others but also to forgive myself. I want to choose her God over everything else."

With that you sat down and listened while others said basically the same. One woman had changed the hearts of so many that day. This whole room of so-called gangsters would never be the same. This lady had finally given her husband's death to God so a room full of prisoners could be set free.

This week of prison turned out to be the longest ever. Your anticipation of the final class that Mrs. Thomas would present could not get here quick enough. Every inmate involved in the class could talk about nothing else. You noticed the great calm that had fallen upon the prison and you wished it would never end. This was the first class in this prison's history that had never lost a student due to disciplinary reasons. That stat was amazing within itself; but what was more incredible was the fact that this class consisted of some of the most hardcore prisoners in the system, and yet, not one of the fifty-five inmates had received a write up from security for misbehavior. What was it about this class? What was it about this woman? Those questions whirled around in every inmate's head, and not just those in class. Every gang-banger had seen a difference in their comrades. And the time just ticked by so slowly.

Then the day arrived: and finally, the hour. When class was called out, not one person was late. Everyone sat waiting for the entry of Mrs. Thomas; and who walked in with her, but the old Judge himself. Mrs. Thomas introduced him, told of how they became friends, and how he had recently retired and wanted to see what this class was all about. She said she was proud to know such a great man. With that, she sat down and the Judge began to speak. He talked about your day in court, and how his life had changed that day. He spoke about the compassion Mrs. Thomas had shown to you and your family, and how she had melted the heart of every person in the courtroom that day. He also talked about having to end court early that day, because he found himself letting too many people off scot-free.

The whole class laughed and he smiled, and then continued. "Mrs. Thomas truly changed my life that day; I met Jesus. After court, she came to my office and led me to the Lord. I didn't think I needed anything in life, but I needed a Savior. I thank God she entered into my life before it was too late. I can't begin to tell you how many people in my life had tried to tell me about Jesus. But she did more than tell; she lived it. So, here I am today, seeing the great work the Lord is still having her do. I am so proud to know her, and so proud to have been introduced to her favorite friend, Jesus Himself. Thank you."

The entire class stood and clapped. Mrs. Thomas rose to her feet and took the platform. "I hope you still feel like this when this class is over. So here we go. Today is your day of reckoning. Are you going to change for the better or for the worse? When I say this, I want to make sure you hear this, so I am going to say it twice. Oh, who knows, maybe ten times before I leave today." She paused and shouted, "You are not the victim; do you hear me? You are not the victim! The victim is the person you robbed, beat, shot, or killed. The victim is the person or persons you did harm to. The victim is the loved ones left behind. You're not them. Are you listening? Quit acting like the victim! You are the victimizer! You are the manipulator! You are the one who ruined someone else's life. Have you got that? Listen, don't ever act like the victim again. That is not who you are!"

With that, everyone was frozen in their seats. No one knew if she was done yelling and ready to start throwing stuff, or what. What everyone did know was that we were not the victims, never had been by her definition, and it was our place to change and not anyone else's. She began to speak softly and slowly, "Today, all pity parties are over with. You do not have a right to a pity party. Oh poor me! If that's your response, then you haven't learned a thing. You have a couple of rights, and that's it. You have a right to ask for forgiveness, and if the victim doesn't have it within himself or herself to do such, then learn to forgive yourself, with God's help, of course, and move on with your life. Accept the change that God has made available and learn to walk in His grace. Remember what grace is; it is unmerited favor. It is a gift; you cannot do anything to earn it. Do you understand? The hardest thing you will ever deal with is learning to forgive yourself. Listen, don't try to figure God out; just trust that He cares for you and wants a relationship with His creation. Did you get that? He wants a relationship with you. Someone else can't fulfill this for you. You've got to do it yourself. It's yours and His relationship. I pray you get what I have."

She walked silently back to her set, and then the Governor and the Commissioner of Corrections entered into the room. They each stood at the podium and talked about what a remarkable woman Mrs. Thomas was. They both spoke about what she had said to the Governor the first day the class started, and how they were embarrassed to have tried to get credit for this class. They both apologized to her and asked if she would consider presenting this class to other prisoners across the State. She nodded her approval and continued to listen. The Commissioner told her what a remarkable change had occurred in this prison, and that not one inmate in this class had received a disciplinary report during the five weeks of this course. He also told her not one fight had occurred during the same period of time. This prison had gone from being the most violent in the State, to having the least amount of disciplinaries amongst all State Prisons within the last five weeks. "Nothing whatsoever could be responsible for this change except you and your class, Mrs. Thomas, and you are welcomed back anytime. Thank you."

With that, every inmate, the Judge, the Commissioner and the Governor gave her a standing ovation.

And the class was over. One special person forever changed that prison; a woman who should have been dead for months now. But she wasn't, she was alive and well, and giving inmates reasons to live, and teaching her cause. If only you had counted the costs of having one more drink. At least you now knew what it meant to count the costs of doing anything again, or for that matter, not doing what you should. Would you have sufficient to finish what had been started?

Chapter Nine

Changes

Now that class was over, changes started taking place in your life: physical changes anyway. You wanted to change, so you started with friends first. The set of prisoners you had met in class became the people you associated with the most. There were only a few in the dorm you were assigned to, but you got to know each of them pretty well; and within the next two months, more were assigned into the dorm. Your cellmate was cool with all of them, so the dorm actually became a safe haven inside the prison.

Your cellmate became popular among your new friends because they had the ability to change gang tattoos into just regular old tattoos. Within weeks, not even security could identify your body markings as gang related anymore, and neither could other inmates. You disassociated with all your old gang members, or at least you thought you did. Most of your old gang had been moved to other dorms or other prisons. This new group of friends helped pass the time by. You actually started going to chapel call. Still, your change was only physical, maybe a little mental and emotional, but nothing spiritual yet. A couple of the class members had actually accepted Christ Jesus as their Lord and Savior, and you were okay with that.

Then the inevitable happened. Your cellmate was transferred to another prison. You hated that; you would now have to get use to another person becoming your roommate, your confidant. That was one of the hardest things about prison, learning to trust another human being that you had nothing to do with the choosing. Would they be like you? Would they be your race, your nationality? Could you get along? Would you have the same basic belief system?

You were stressed for days and had not even been able to enjoy being in a cell by yourself.

And then here this person appeared. They looked straight, looked happy-go-lucky, and stayed to themselves for the first few weeks just getting a feel for you and the rest of the inmates. Each of you had exchanged casual words, but had not gotten to know each other as of yet. Your dorm mates took to your cellmate before you did. They began to open up to them way before you did, and vice versa. Finally one day, you asked what brought them to prison. They shared their story and basically their life history. You were almost sorry you asked, as they went on and on. But you listened anyway.

After days of comparing lives and stories, you felt pretty good about your roommate. You began to share like you had been friends for years, and came to find out that you had actually attended the same grammar school. You thought that was kind of neat, so before long, you had a best friend.

Not sure what it was, but this new best friend had become a vital part of your class group that still met weekly in the dorm concerning the class Mrs. Thomas taught. It was just like they had been a part of that class. It was almost confusing to you. Were they in there and you just didn't know it? No, you knew they had come from a different prison. Oh well, they fit right in, so you stopped giving it any more thought.

So life went on for months, no troubles whatsoever, so you felt confident you could tell this person anything. One night while you should have been sleeping, each of you shared about the bad things you had done in prison to survive. They shared with you about all the fights they had been involved in while in prison, so you thought nothing of it when you shared how you had been forced to join a gang. So here you are sharing with this person you only met months earlier, about the hate gang you had joined. That gang had taken revenge on inmates who had beaten you. You share how you found yourself stabbing other gang members to prove your loyalty to the gang. You can't seem to hush, so you leave out no detail. You even tell your roommate why you never got caught; and for some stupid reason, you tell them where you always hid your weapon.

That was your demise. Within weeks, this new roommate was gone. And within just a couple of months, you found yourself being locked down and indicted for attempted murder, three times over. You realized you had been set up, brought down by the State Police. This so-called roommate that you had gotten so close to was an undercover officer. You didn't know there was such a thing in prison, and you had trusted this person. Life just kept getting tougher and tougher, and then it dawned on you, you had not counted the costs of running your mouth.

Within hours of being locked down, you were transported to superior court, made your first court appearance, met with a public defender, and found just how serious these new charges were. Within just a few minutes after arriving, you found yourself being transported back to prison segregation.

This was the second time your mouth had gotten you indicted, as you looked backed. First for taking in one more drink, and then, running into and killing someone. And now this; running your mouth to someone you had only just met, and telling your most intimate prison secrets. How stupid could you get? Could you ever trust anyone again?

How about yourself? Time would tell.

You write to your spouse and tell them of your new troubles, knowing this will probably be the end of your marriage. You lay your head down and fall asleep.

You stay in segregation for more than sixty days, and then, out of the blue, you get a visit.

Chapter Ten

The State's deal

The CERT team escorts you to an area of the prison which you have never seen. In this room are several well-dressed individuals, numerous State Police in fatigues, and a video camera set up to record the meeting. You do not like this. The CERT team instructs you that once you are seated, you are not to get up for any reason. With that, the CERT team exits the room and one of the well-dressed men starts to introduce everyone there. You find there are numerous agencies represented here; but you also notice, no one is representing you. You ask the State Attorney that was introduced first if she thought you needed an attorney present for this meeting. She advised you that if you felt you did, then that was your prerogative, but that wasn't why they were here. They were here, she said, to get your help in a situation; and if the information was what they believed to be true, then your charges would be done away with, abolished, as far as they were concerned. With that, they begin to explain their need for your services.

The attorney, whose name was Ms. Smith, explained how your charges would go away if you cooperated with the State Police and the federal agencies investigating a certain inmate in one of the other prisons located within thirty miles of your home town. She said if you agreed to help the authorities, then all of this could take place within days. She explained the danger of the assignment, and also explained the risk was too great for an officer to carry out this mission. She even related to you that it was a retired judge and the Governor of the State, who recommended you for such an assignment.

This was the reason they were here, and that was all she could and would say until you either accepted or rejected the deal. With that offer, she sat down, and not a word was spoken for over ten minutes.

Finally, you began to speak, and not even you could believe what came out of your mouth. You explained to the entire group how you had gone through a class about learning to count the costs in everything you did. You explained how you had failed at this class by believing that a new cellmate was who they actually said they were. And now you were being asked to do almost the same thing, getting information on another inmate, and you weren't even an officer. You told them you would need time to think about this, maybe even get advice from someone other than an attorney or a relative.

One of the State Police officers interrupted you and asked if you meant Mrs. Thomas, and without hesitation, you said yes. With that, everyone there stood to their feet, said arrangements would be made, and the room was cleared within seconds. You were left alone, and you prayed no employee at this prison heard a word that was said. The CERT team arrived within a few minutes and escorted you back to segregation. You would remain there for another sixty days, but this time, you had remembered to count the costs.

One morning, very early, four o'clock to be exact, the CERT team woke you and escorted you back to that same room where you had met the State Attorney and the other officers from several agencies. And there sat Mrs. Thomas, looking as bright as the sunshine. She said she was happy to see you and asked if you were ready to talk about counting the costs. You advised her you already had, and that you had done it right this time. She smiled and said, "You know it was me who recommended you for this mission, don't you?" With that, you told her that you had finally figured it out. She smiled and said, "So what is your answer?" You told her that you knew you would be receiving a minimum of seven years to run consecutively for each case, and you knew you could not survive another twenty-one years in prison and think your spouse wouldn't leave you, so you would do whatever the State wanted, if, she would give you what she had. You wanted a relationship with Christ. You just wanted Mrs. Thomas' advice as to whether you were doing the right thing or not, and you knew she could hear the Lord's voice.

With that, she told you how to have a relationship with God, and she shared with you that you had to acknowledge that you were in need of a Savior, ask for forgiveness of your sins, and believe that Jesus went to the cross for that very purpose. And if you confessed with your mouth the Lord Jesus, and believed in your heart that God raised Him from the dead, then you would be saved. And right then and there, you were. You were forever changed on the inside; your spirit had received life.

She then assured you that from what little information she had received about this individual in prison, if they weren't stopped, then there could be several deaths within months both inside and outside the prison, and she stressed again that time was the enemy. The State needed someone on the inside to assist, and you were their best chance in getting such information. She explained that once you signed on, she would be starting a Counting the Costs Class at the prison you would be assigned to, and you would be a part of the class, because, she was your victim. All of this made sense, and you felt better, but her next words were great to hear. She said, "Your spouse told me to tell you, they are not going anywhere, they are waiting with open arms. For better or for worse, remember? And yes, just a few months ago while attending a Bible study at my house, your spouse renewed their relationship with God. We have been praying for you ever since; and look at what prayer has done. Our God is so faithful!" With that, and tears flowing down her face, she was out the door. You found yourself back in segregation before anyone else had awakened.

Within days, you were once again escorted out of segregation early in the morning before any other inmate awoke. You found yourself once again in the room with the same group that had offered you the State's deal if you agreed to help them. Once again, they were all introduced to you. This time, when Ms. Smith spoke, she introduced another attorney who would be your handler, and for now own, this person would become your personal attorney, therefore protecting you and the State concerning confidentiality. It was explained to you that this would be the only time you would see any of these other people again. You acknowledged that you understood.

Ms. Smith and Mr. Davis, your handler, began to lay out the reasons the State needed help with this case. The inmate in questioned, had been a narcotics officer for over five years in another State and a corrections officer for the State Prison system here for three years. It was believed they had sold drugs and provided other contraband to gang leaders and given special protection both outside and inside the prison system. It was believed they had protection themselves provided by every gang known in this State. It was thought that this individual was responsible for contraband being introduced into every prison, including the one you were about to enter. It was a known fact that this officer had arranged at least ten murders while working street narcotics. This was one dangerous person.

Mr. Davis went on to explain how this inmate had now been assigned to a prison where corrupt officers and convicted State dignitaries were incarcerated. No one there could be trusted, not even the officers who worked there. It would be up to you to get as much information on this individual as possible without getting yourself killed.

It was also explained to you that not one soul knew Mr. Davis had anything to do with the State. Mr. Davis would simply be your attorney working on your new charges. It was not unusual for an attorney to visit his client every four or five months, so that was how this would be handled. There would be no letters, absolutely nothing to tie you to the State.

Federal authorities explained their interests were in the murders only, since on several occasions, the crimes had crossed State lines. They asked you if you felt comfortable involving yourself in such a case. You said, "Not really, but I'll take my chances. Don't expect rapid results, I'm living one day at a time, and that's it. I'm not making any promises; I'm just going to let this person open up to me if they wish. That's it."

Ms. Smith spoke up and said, "That's all we can ask. The prisoner you will be housed with is Inmate Pat Francis. Remember, we think this is the most dangerous inmate of their gender in the State system. Be careful."

And with that, the meeting was over; and within just a few minutes, you were escorted back to your cell by the CERT team. Again, not one inmate was aware that you had ever left your cell.

Within just a few days, you were being loaded onto a bus headed to the Diagnostic Center, where transfers took place. You were so thankful you had survived that prison. What would this new prison be like? Only time would tell.

Chapter Eleven

A new beginning

Once you were put into belly chains and leg-irons, you boarded the bus and immediately recognized several of your old dorm mates. It was like a reunion. Everyone was wondering if the prison would ever let you out of segregation. You laughed, told every one of them how nice it had been, not having to deal with any other inmates, so everyone had a good laugh. Everybody on the bus was betting on where each other would end up; but only you knew where you were really headed. Everyone had heard that you had new charges you were facing, so they all sympathized with you, and wished you the best of luck. You shared with each of them that while you were locked down, you had finally accepted Jesus as your Lord and Savior. A few of them were actually happy for you; but most said it would only last for a season, and then you would be back with them. Everybody had another good laugh, and you prayed what they were saying wouldn't be true. You wanted this relationship with Jesus to last forever. You shared with all of the inmates on the bus that you had almost read through the whole Bible since being in segregation. Again, the roar of laughter filled the bus; and then silence fell, and the ride was quiet for the next two hours.

Once you reached the transfer center, it dawned on you that this was the place you had received your first prison stitches. That seemed so long ago, and you hoped that never happened again. There were several officers waiting for the arrival of your bus, as it was the last to reach the transfer station. All inmates said their good-byes, and as quick as you had arrived, you were loaded onto another bus to be delivered to your new home for the next several months. This time when you entered the bus, you recognized not one person. And this ride was like your original ride from the Diagnostic Center to the first permanent prison, which you had stayed for the last twenty-four months; it was so quiet you could hear yourself sweat. And sweat you did; your nerves got the best of you. Fear gripped you like it was your best friend. It would not let go. If you could have, you would have jumped off this bus, even while it was moving. You took several deep breaths, and finally calmed down enough to finish out the ride. The bus had pulled into numerous prisons along the way, and finally, you noticed only two other inmates left on the bus; and there you were, at your new living quarters.

Intake was a little more relaxed at this prison, and there were only five hundred inmates assigned: a vast difference from the last institution. Orientation was different also, as the three of you who entered the prison together, were orientated at the same time. You thought that this place might not be so bad, and then you were escorted to your dormitory.

This was different, not one person had a detail. In fact, you were told by your dorm officer, not one inmate could be trusted here. All inmates were former law enforcement, ex-judges, or former dignitaries of the State or County governments. Every person here had gone through high profile court cases, and was found to be untrustworthy. The dorm officer told you not to get involved with any of them, as each person here was a user of other people. With that short speech, you were escorted to your cell and locked in with your new roommate.

And there sat Pat Francis. You knew nothing else to do but introduce yourself, and all they did was say hello. No other words were spoken between the two of you for more than a week. You had met many other inmates, even several ex-officers from your hometown. To say the least, this was one laid back prison. You even found out your dorm had a prayer group that met twice a week, so you immediately joined. This was the safest you had felt in prison since the first day you arrived in the system. You were beginning to love this place, and then your cellmate started talking. They questioned you over and over as to why you were assigned to this prison, and especially this particular dorm. You opened up to them and began to tell them that you were part of a new class that was going to be taught here. It was a part of victim impact and the person teaching the class was your victim, well, in a sort. They were the victim left behind, as you had killed their spouse, by accident of course, and now, wherever the class was taught, you were assigned so you could be an active participant in the class. It was for the victim, you said, so they could fully express what you had done to their family, and for that matter the family you had left behind; and it was for the inmates so they could learn to count the costs of what they had done. You started to talk a little more and your new roommate cut you off and said, "I've heard all I want to hear. We all got wind of this class several months ago, and we all have been told we have to go through it. Enjoy this place while you are here, but stay out of my business. I do my time by myself. Understand?" You said you did; and with that it was another several weeks before the two of you spoke again.

You could tell your cellmate studied you like a hawk. They were forever going behind you and asking others what you all had discussed. Some of the inmates had little idea who your cellmate was, so they explained that if they wanted to be part of a conversation, then all they had to do was join in. So within just another few weeks, your roommate started opening up to the dorm. Knowing almost every person here were former cops, your roommate had reason to be paranoid. Your roommate knew these other inmates were trained in investigations, and they trusted no one. You were the only inmate assigned to this dorm that wasn't involved in some type of government work. So somewhere along the line, they began to trust you, and they began to share different stories of their life with you. One reason they did this was to see if you would tell any other inmate; and another reason was they just didn't have anyone else to talk with. You knew this was the way your last cellmate had entrapped you, so you dared not discuss your conversations with anyone else. In fact, whatever conversation you had in the dorm with whichever inmate it was, was never shared with any other inmate.

You had learned a great lesson here. Your business was yours and yours only. And that applied to everyone. People started putting more faith in you every day. You were someone the whole dorm could share with without fearing someone would run their mouth. The whole dorm could see your relationship with God was for real. You liked the person you were becoming.

Before long, the first class with Mrs. Thomas began. Fifty inmates were assigned, but your cellmate was not in the first class. The same excitement that you experienced in the first class you ever attended was the same excitement that was stirred in this prison. All inmates could talk about was this new class. So many other type classes had been taught before, but having a victim teach a class opened the eyes of every person involved. They could see their own crime unfold, and the victims left behind. With this class you became a celebrity amongst your peers, in a negative way of course. You had ruined a person's dreams, and your victim did not mind telling her full story. You were the cause of this new program, and yet the change in you had helped you face the consequences of the poor decisions you had made in life. Not one inmate in class envied you; none of them ever wanted their story told. But you handled it well, and your roommate noticed that you were the kind of person they would choose as a friend, if they were out on the street. You were also one of the few inmates that needed nothing in the way of drugs to survive incarceration. To your cellmate, you had it all together. So they began to share more of their life stories with you. You played it different though; you told them you didn't trust who they were, and that you were okay not knowing anything about them. You knew this would just make them more curious about you. And you were right. You found out they had inquired through their correctional officer friends if you were who you said you were. You got this information from other inmates who did not care for your cellmate. They advised you that your cellmate owned numerous of the officers at this prison. Several officers were on your cellmate's payroll. That put fear in you; so you decided to do the right thing and deal with your cellmate directly. You waited till the lights went out, and then you addressed your roommate with the following question. "Are you inquiring about me through other inmates? Why don't you just come to me if you have a problem with who I am? I don't need anybody wondering if I have told them the truth. I have been honest with you. If you want to know something about me, then ask me. Don't ever go behind my back again. Do you understand?" With that, neither you nor your roommate spoke another word to each other for the next two days. You wondered where this boldness had come from. You wondered if you should fear for your life, but you just weren't afraid of anyone anymore. Your life had changed, and it had to be because of Jesus.

Ms. Thomas' class continued to make an impact on the inmates at this prison. The entire classes' theme was that this teaching should have been taught while they were at the academies or at law school. Most participants stated that if such a course existed in their early careers, just maybe they would have not ended up behind bars. Your words were, "I wished that before I had ever taken my first drink, someone would have told me that prison would be my destiny if drinking was my answer to all of my problems." Everyone agreed that this class was enlightening.

You had almost come to think that this class was the only reason for your being at this prison; and then one day out of the blue, your roommate suddenly started being more friendly to you. They advised you that they had learned that you had outstanding charges for attempted murder hanging over your head, and if there was anything they could do for you in regards to your case, all you needed to do was ask. You knew that you had not shared that information with anyone at this prison, so you took advantage of this conversation by asking, "Just how did you come to this conclusion? I have not shared that part of my life with anyone here. I already told you to ask me directly if there is something you want to know about me. My business is not yours!" With that, you exited your cell and went to the dayroom to cool down. You knew this was a window of opportunity to finally get your cellmate to open up about who they really were. Your little outburst worked perfectly. Within minutes, your roommate was there apologizing and asking if they could speak to you in private. With that, you got up and went to the control room and asked the officer if it was okay if the two of you could go out to the dorm recreation yard for some air. The officer electronically unlocked the dorm door, and you and Inmate Francis went out.

The two of you were the only inmates on the yard, so at least each of you could talk without anyone else around. And talk they did; in fact, you learned more about this individual in an hour's time than you had learned in months. You had actually played it just right. They told you about their careers, both as a police officer and as a correctional officer. They explained that their greed had gotten them noticed by their supervisors in the police force; thus before getting busted, they changed careers and became a CO, (a Corrections Officer). They explained their connections with drug dealers and gang members had opened an influx of money into their lives like never before. They explained that their addictive behavior had led to this life of crime that was impossible to escape.

"So," they said, "If you can't get away from it, then why not just run it. This is what I am best at. I own at least two percent of the officers that work for the State Corrections Department. I make sure they are paid more money than corrections could ever pay them; in fact, I did the same on the street when working narcotics. Every narcotics agent in my department was on my payroll. I knew about every bust, so the other agents and I could take care of certain gang members and make sure our enterprise thrived. I got busted in prison because I failed to follow my own rules; I screwed up and got caught with contraband in one of my own vehicles. Several officers, narcotic agents and corrections officers, turned State evidence against me and got sweet deals; but I have taken care of those matters since. I know the system backwards and forwards; and right now I have enough people working within the system that I can retire when I leave this prison. Most of these people can be bought since the State pays so little. Oh, and how I got a hold of your records, not just officers need cash. I had a counselor run your history for me. Have I said enough?"

You looked right into their eyes and said, "With all the crooked officers and dignitaries here, how in the world do you know who to trust? If I were you, I would not trust a soul." Their answer didn't surprise you. "With the folks who work for me, I can find anyone's most intimate secret. All it takes is my people inside and outside doing what I tell them to do. They already know that if they fail me or think they can cheat me, their end is just around the corner. I make sure it is instilled in them: first screw-up, usually their last."

You cut them off immediately and say, "No!" They ask you what you are talking about. You say again, "No, there is nothing you can do for me. I don't want any help with my case. I am perfectly all right with facing the court. I think my odds with the courts are better with me staying alive than with me getting in debt with you."

The two of you had a good laugh concerning your answer, but you assured them you were serious. You again emphasized the seriousness of your answer. "I promise I will take my chances with the court. I have made it this far by myself; thanks anyway, but no thanks."

With that, over the next several months, the two of you become pretty good friends, but you know you can never trust this person. Every time they bring up your case, you cut them off immediately and tell them you need nothing from them. You stress to them you like having a friend in prison, but you don't like the kind of help they are offering. You tell them that just like they need nothing from you, you need nothing from them. "Let's just be friends," you say.

More than two sets of inmates have completed victim impact classes and still your cellmate has yet to attend. And then, one rainy morning, they get notice that they are assigned to the next class. Your only thought is, "Will they really learn what it means to count the costs of what they have done?" And then that fear that you haven't felt for a while visits you and says, "Have you counted the costs of what you have been asked to do: really counted it?"

Within minutes, you are notified that you have an attorney visit waiting. Your cellmate looks up at you from their bunk and says, "You sure you don't want my help? My offer still stands." As you walk out the door, you say, "Not even." You both laugh, but you know your laugh isn't real. You hope your cellmate doesn't pick up on your fear.

Chapter Twelve

Mr. Davis' visit

This is the first time you have been to the attorney visit area at this prison. In fact, you realize you know very little about the physical plant of this prison. Not much inmate movement happens here. You don't feel very comfortable about this visit, so you just stare at Mr. Davis with a helpless victim expression. He knows what that means, so he pulls out a stack of forms, and starts talking about your case. As he talks, you begin to read the questions he has written in number 4 pencil on each of the form sheets. Number 4 pencil can barely be seen with the naked eye up close, much less by anyone or anything from any distance. The first question is this; "Do you think we are being listened to?" You answer the first question by checking the appropriate box. The next question reads, "Do you see any cameras recording this meeting?" He continues to talk as you casually look around the room. When you have checked the room thoroughly, you check the box, which reads, 'yes.' He continues to talk and pulls out a new form package. He removes the old forms from the table and places them back in his briefcase. He calls out for an officer; and within seconds, an officer appears, opens the door, and asks, "Are you finished?" Mr. Davis says no, and request that anyone with a notary stamp please be summoned. The officer exits the room, and again Mr. Davis pulls out a sheet of paper. It reads as follows; "Percentage involved?" You write nothing, but instead, you rub your lips with two fingers. Mr. Davis appears bewildered, not because you didn't write it down, but that he sees that as a high figure. He speaks to you and says, "This is a 300 page document I am submitting to the courts in your behalf." You know what that means; there are over three hundred employees in the prison system working for your cellmate. That is a huge number. You and Mr. Davis both know there is no one in the system that can be trusted.

A very young lady steps inside the room and ask to see the documents Mr. Davis needs to have notarized. He pulls out what looks to be ream of paper, has you to sign the back sheet, and the young lady both signs and seals the document. Mr. Davis thanks her and then ask, "Why are there cameras in an area where there is supposed to be attorney, client privilege?" She politely answers, "The attorney's rooms are being painted today and we are sorry for the inconvenience; this is an interview room for investigative purposes." Mr. Davis knows what that means; this was all a set-up, and he is ever so grateful that nothing was said that could be used against you. His eye contact and body language says it all.

The two of you sit a little longer and just chat about the weather, life on the outside, and the years you are facing. You ask him about mutual friends, and he lets you know everything is okay.

As he gets up to exit, you know you probably won't be hearing back from him until you have been transferred from this prison. It's just too dangerous.

Chapter Thirteen

Lessons interrupted

You are happy you are doing this class with Mrs. Thomas. It has truly passed the time in prison for you. You can't even imagine what it is like for some of the inmates who do nothing but sit around. You feel sorry for them, because, they have nothing to look forward to, even when their time is finally complete. They are dead inside, and have little to no hope. You are so glad for your new relationship with God. You know that if it weren't for that, you would probably be in the grave. You remember how it felt when you were living without one glimmer of hope. Those days are over for you; you have life and you want others to accept what you have received from God.

You've come to the point that, every morning when you arise, you thank God for letting you be assigned to this prison. It has been great for your family also. They have been able to see you more in the past few months than they saw you in the first two years of your incarceration. It is great being close to home. The way the Counting the Costs class is going, you could be here until your time is up, unless something in Mrs. Thomas' schedule changes. You like what this class has done to the inmates who have completed it. They are more open, more receptive, and just happier people in general. Also from that class, more and more inmates in your dorm are joining Bible study. You look how far you have come and admit to yourself, you haven't even scratched the surface yet. You know there is a lifetime of learning ahead.

After returning from evening chow call, your roommate says they have something to discuss with you. You tell them it is almost Bible study time and ask if it can wait. They say if you don't mind, it's really important. So you do what any good roommate would do; you sit down and give your full attention to you cellmate. They say, "I have a problem, I think one of the other inmates in the dorm is investigating me; there have been a couple of my former co-workers busted in the last few days. They were close friends, if you know what I mean. I'm worried for my safety, as word has been passed to me that a hit might have been put out by some of my old friends. Do you think you can snoop around and see if you hear anything related to me? You don't know what it is like being around a bunch of former cops who don't care for drug dealing ex-officers. I might be in over my head here. Since this new class has started, more and more of these people want to do the right thing, whatever that means. Do you mind helping me out?" You assure them that they are just paranoid, as not one word has been mentioned about them to you or around you. That still doesn't suffice their conscience. So you say, "Look, I'll do everything in my power to see if there is any cause for you to worry any more about this situation. I still think you are just paranoid, but I have an idea. Why don't you go to the dayroom with me, and just sit and listen to Bible study? It might change your thinking about who you are serving time with; some of these folks have become God fearing people." They pause and say, "I'll borrow your words. Thanks, but no thanks." You both laugh and you tell them that you have their back. They smile and you go on to Bible study.

When you finally returned to your cell, your roommate asked if you wanted to learn what it really meant to be an officer in a prison. You said sure, and for the next five weeks, Inmate Francis taught you all about prison and its work force. "Here's the deal," they said. "If you help me to learn to really count the costs of what I have done in life, then you will become the most knowledgeable inmate besides me at this prison concerning the workings of the State Department of Corrections." You said okay, went and showered, and got ready for bed, because tomorrow Mrs. Thomas' class would begin.

Morning came early, as you didn't sleep very well. Something about your roommate telling you that there might be a hit on them made you fear for your safety. Could there actually be a contract on their life? From what you knew, there could be more than one. This person had not made very good decisions since getting involved in law enforcement. There was a possibility that someone wanted your cellmate's business inside the prison; someone who wasn't incarcerated and went to their home every day, someone who was tired of making little bucks, and wanted more. Who knew? It could be any officer there. Officers were capable of bringing in contraband, so a weapon could be brought into a prison and used against anyone, including your roommate; for that matter, you.

After chow you quickly got ready for class and so did your roommate. Several other inmates were already seated when you arrived at the classroom. You noticed Mrs. Thomas was trying to put on a happy face; but just knowing her as you did, you didn't think she was feeling well. As the rest of the inmates arrived, you were careful to make sure you were not bringing attention to yourself, as you knew this was her class, not yours.

Mrs. Thomas taught the class the same way she had done for the last three classes, and had yet to pull out one note. The class was amazed that the financial costs were so much, and several inmates spoke up and thanked her for showing them how to face up to what their crimes had costs their families and themselves. Not one person in class had ever gotten that far in trying to figure out what they had lost, dollar wise. You tried not to, but you watched your roommate to see if they had any reaction at all, but you could not detect any emotion from their face whatsoever. When class was over, one inmate asked you, "How do you go through this each time? I would just die." The rest of the class concurred with them. You explained that it wasn't pleasant, but that for your life to mean something, it was absolutely necessary. This was a time in your life that you could heal, and you were taking full advantage of it. With that, security escorted the inmates back to their dorms, and this time, there were no strip searches. That was a first and that was strange. Never in any prison or jail had you gone anywhere that you were not strip searched, other than chow. Even every class that had taken place at this prison before was subjected to strip searches; so why not this one? Then you thought, maybe your cellmate had moved some kind of contraband during the class and his cohorts inside the department knew not to conduct shakedowns. Whatever it was, it was strange. You didn't dare say one word to anyone else about this.

When you arrived back at the dorm, your roommate informed you that they too would be giving you your first lesson on prison workers after chow. You said you couldn't wait, and they smiled for the first time all day long. You knew they were fearful and that they needed someone to just talk to.

As chow ended, they caught up with you on the sidewalk and asked if you wanted to stay on the dorm yard instead of going into the dorm. You said, "That sounds good;" so the two of you remained on the rec yard while everyone else went back inside the dorm. The weather was pleasant; so for the next three hours you got your first lesson on folks who worked in prison, and it was almost more information than you could contain.

Pat informed you that Corrections was the hardest of all law enforcement jobs to work. There was no glory in it whatsoever. There were no pats on the back, and most workers felt alone all the time. "Your post is your post," they said, "and you cannot leave it for any reason without permission from your supervisor; and what that means is you can be stuck in one place for more than a shift if your replacement decides not to come to work, and that happens more than you would believe. So what happens? You find you are just a body occupying a space. You find no one seems to care, and you find inmates use this against you to reel you in; and pretty soon, you find that you relate better with inmates than with your co-workers. You have become a victim of manipulation, and you either do what the inmates tell you, quit, get fired, or you become an inmate yourself. That happens to about two percent of staff within their first year of employment. That is why you see new officers all the time. That's how I got other employees on my payroll; I listened to their complaints, saw their discouragement, and showed them how they could make more money than they ever thought about. That is also the reason I am an inmate now; my greed overtook me. I just couldn't get enough. It was the same on the street; money became my god."

You looked at Pat very hard and then spoke up. "So why are you telling me this? You know I have changed my life and want no part of this." "I know," they said, "but I wanted you to know how hard it is for these people to maintain their integrity. Their starting salaries are almost poverty level; and with a family, it is so easy for them to be sucked into whatever scheme is being played against them. Listen, very little about the con is being taught in the academy, so these officers aren't equipped to withstand the pressure unless they truly have a good set of morals and values. Don't get me wrong, most do; and a good percentage retire from Corrections, but it's the young ones that you can manipulate and get them to do your dirty work. That is why I'm sitting here today; I entered dirty and continued in my sin. Isn't that what Mrs. Thomas called it?"

With that, you knew you could change the subject. "So you got nothing out of that class today? You didn't hear a word other than sin? Did you not hear what she taught about counting the costs of what you had done to others?" Pat stopped you again and said, "Believe me, I got it. I think it is just too late for me to change. Did you not hear what I said to you today? I not only think there is a contract out on me, it was confirmed to me during class. Did you not wonder why we weren't strip searched today after class? It's because one of my officers passed the name of the assailant to me that I must avoid. At least that person isn't in our dorm, but they are in our class. Security figures since there were no searches today, just maybe, that person will bring their weapon next time and get caught with it. That's what I am hoping. I don't want someone to have to take this person out, because, this crime would be tied to me. I can't afford that. And again, yes, I got plenty out of Mrs. Thomas' class. And yes, I agree with the rest of the class; I don't know how you do it, but I am glad you do. You are the only person I can trust here. Now on another subject, do you see how bad it is for these officers? Can you imagine being married to one of them, the heartache they must go through daily? I would not want the pressure of wondering if my spouse was going to make it home every day, or wondering if they were going to do something wrong and get themselves busted. That's what these folks go through every day. On top of that, even if they are good people, they still have to prove themselves to staff every moment of every day. Law enforcement is the only job, besides military, of course, that you have to prove yourself on a daily basis, and risk your life every moment of every day. What you did yesterday counts for nothing; today is what counts in Corrections." With those words you see an opening to witness to Pat. "What you just said is also Biblical; yesterday doesn't count anymore. That's the past. There is nothing you can do about your past, but repent. You can't change what has already happened. We also need to live for today and not worry about what can happen tomorrow, because there is enough evil in the world right now that faces you and I." Your roommate interrupts and says, "Amen to that." You both laugh, but you know you made your point. You also know they heard it loud and clear. You both go back towards the dorm feeling pretty good. Pat whispers to you, "Still, keep your ears open; I don't trust anyone here." You smile and whisper back, "Well it is prison." By the time the dorm door is unlocked, you both are laughing hysterically. Everyone is glad to see the two of you getting along. You think to yourself about Mrs. Thomas and the peace she seems to bring every time she visits the prison. You thank God for meeting her, and you thank Him for the forgiveness she has shown to you and your family, and you thank God for Jesus.

The rest of the week flies by for some unknown reason. You do what Pat asked; you listen to see if their name is mentioned by anyone. Not one soul says anything concerning them, so you prepare yourself for the next class. This one is always your hardest. You seem to always learn something else about the troubles you have caused your family. You hope this next class will be different, no troubles revealed.

Week two of Counting the Costs Class arrives, but Mrs. Thomas doesn't. All the members of the class are notified that it will resume the next week; but no information is available as to why she missed today. You are concerned and you hope everything is okay with her health. You mope the entire week and no one can do anything to console you. You pretty much stay away from your roommate as much as possible, and when visitation comes, your spouse doesn't show up either. Now you begin to worry, and you haven't done that in a while. You begin to think of all the things that could keep them away. You realize you have given little thought to family this week; your thinking has been focused on Mrs. Thomas the entire time.

You're so thankful when class is called out. You try your best to be the first inmate there, but by the time you arrive, the class is almost full. You find yourself having to be like all of the other class; if Mrs. Thomas wants you to know anything about last week, then you will all learn about it together.

As week two class begins, she says she is sorry she missed last week, but something more important came up. She said, "I had to help out a friend. I had to conduct a funeral. It's one of the hardest things a minister has to do, especially when it's someone you have grown close to." She looks right at you and says, "One of the things about not counting the costs in life is, sometimes you get left out of knowing when loved ones pass from this life to eternity. Last week we buried your spouse's father. He died of a heart attack. It was sudden, not even a warning. He wasn't sick or anything. He was out for a walk and just died. Your spouse agreed not to tell you; they wanted me to share it with you and the class, so every one of you can see how not counting the costs of what you do can have such an effect on you and others around you. We notified the prison system of the death, but since they would not allow you to attend, your spouse left it up to me to tell you. They thought the impact would have that much more meaning, especially amongst your fellow inmates. Look, I know it's a shock, and if you feel you need to cry right here, I think everyone here would understand. Did you know no one was there to hold your spouse at the funeral? Your children were to overcome with grief to attend. Your spouse had to hold their mother. It was one of the saddest days of my life, so, right in the middle of the funeral, I just stopped and went and held your spouse for you. I cannot believe that not one of you thought of anyone other than yourselves when committing your crimes, even if you were to drunk or too high to remember. All of your families continue to suffer while you just sit here. Look, if you think the separation is tough on you, think about the family you left behind." She stopped long enough to take a deep breath and looked at you square in the eyes and said, "Your spouse needs you. If you ever get out of prison and decide to come back again as an inmate, then you better know I will let you rot in here. I'm not coming back after this five week session anymore. I can't take it. I have already notified the Commissioner that this will be my last group. I'm sorry. It's the unknown that is wearing me out. I wasn't created to do this. I forgave you for what you did to me; but it's hard for me to forgive you for what you have done to your family. I'm struggling, and I am sure you can all see it on my face."

With that being said, class was over. She walked out crying more than you had ever seen her cry before. You sat there in amazement. Each time week two class was taught, something had happened to your family. Your heart was aching, and all you could think about was wanting to hold your spouse. But you couldn't. You would have to wait until they came back to visit. You noticed the class was not making a sound, so you turned around and found everyone just staring at you. You laid your head down on the table and waited until security came in.

When they arrived, you saw a set of tactical officers that you had never seen before. They certainly weren't from this prison. You didn't recognize one of them. They moved every inmate, one by one, into the shakedown room and searched every inch of the facility you were in. What they found scared everyone there, including the administration. A handgun was found in the room in which class had just been conducted. Lockdown was instant, and it remained in place until every one of the security videotapes in that facility were viewed and examined at least five times. Several inmates were locked down, and numerous officers were arrested. It seemed your roommate had escaped detection, but their entire group of corrupt officers, maintenance and kitchen staff and counselors were taken down. You knew you had nothing to do with this, so you now feared that someone was not just watching your roommate, but you also. You couldn't believe what was happening, and neither could Inmate Francis. Security operations didn't return to normal until ten days after the weapon had been found. You were happy to get out of that cell; and when things were back to normal, Pat was happy to start back teaching you the ropes of prison. Neither of you had spoken a word about prison for the last ten days. Anything else was okay to speak about, but not prison nor anyone there.

Inmate Francis finally shared with you that their contacts at this prison had been terminated; not one employee was left that had been on their payroll. Even the young lady that had notarized your legal papers had been fired. You weren't sure what to think, but you knew in your heart that you had nothing to do with this massive termination that was exercised by the Department of Corrections. All you could think of was that you were glad you had not been shot with that gun. And then Inmate Francis spoke up. "That gun was provided to Inmate Johnson, who resided in Dorm G, by Officer Duncan, one of my so-called cohorts. They had wanted to take over my operation after I was locked down several months ago, before you got here; but others had informed on them to me, so Inmate Johnson was paid to kill me. This new class was their best chance, but I put out word so the administration would get wind that there was a gun in the institution. At least I am still alive, even if my operation here has been stopped. There is plenty of time to start another. You will be long gone before my time ends; I'll need something to entertain myself with. Maybe by then, Officer Duncan will be doing time. I can't wait to get my hands on them."

You share with your cellmate the need to pray in private as often as you can. Your cellmate tells you to go for it, and goes down to the dayroom to watch television. You fall to your knees and thank God for protecting you through this ordeal, and you ask Him to protect and comfort your spouse and children. You thank Him for all He does for you, and you pray for your roommate, that they will give their life to Christ. Before closing, you pray for Mrs. Thomas and her family, and you thank God for the class she teaches. You tell Him you know it's selfish, but you hope Mrs. Thomas will change her mind about her desire to stop teaching such an important program. With that, you close and go to the dayroom. And what you find is other inmates witnessing to your cellmate.

Before bed that night, you write to your spouse and tell them how sorry you are that they lost their dad to a heart attack. You share with them how you and the class reacted when everyone learned of your father-in-law's death. You tell your spouse that not being able to hold them in their time of need will forever haunt you, and you ask for forgiveness again. You write, "I pray God will mend our hearts back together again, and forever hold them in His hands." You seal the envelope, and give it to the control room officer so it can be sent out in the morning.

Week three class finally arrived, and you noticed several inmates missing. They had been either locked down or transferred; as they had been a part of the plot to do away with your roommate, or a part of your roommates plot to move contraband throughout the system. Whatever the case, Mrs. Thomas acted as if nothing about the class had changed. This was her day again, and she explained to each inmate that she should have been dead. "Cancer should have killed me," she said, "but because my husband was taken so early in his life, it is my responsibility to tell my grandchildren about the great man he was. No disease will ever stop me from doing that." She shared her courtroom experience, and she shared all of the pain you had caused her and her family. She shared how she had wanted to strangle you, but that God had given her the forgiveness and given her the desire to help other inmates learn to count the costs of what they had done to others and themselves. Her last words of the day were, "Next week, you will learn what forgiveness is all about. I hope you will learn that it is one of the most important life lessons; without it, you can't know God." And then she left, this time smiling.

Shakedown was thorough that day; never before had you been searched by so many officers. As everyone was being escorted back to their dorms, your cellmate said, "Are you ready for your last lesson on prison workers?" You look at them and said, "Sure, but I thought you said it was going to be a five week lesson." Inmate Francis responded, "It has been, you just lost track of time. Just because Mrs. Thomas' class didn't meet every week, doesn't mean ours didn't, even if we didn't talk for ten days straight. Silence in prison is a lesson in itself." You both laugh, enter your dorm, and sit in the dayroom while everyone else is out on the rec yard. Your last lesson begins.

"Did you know that the academy teaches it corrections officers that once they enter the law enforcement field, they automatically lose ten years of their natural life cycle? Do you know why? No, it's not because they average those who get shot or something of that nature into the equation, it's because of the stress that others and ourselves put on our lives. The academies might give a two-minute speech on how to deal with stress, but that is not sufficient. They don't tell you enough about the ups and downs you face on a moment's notice; and they don't tell you that those adrenalin rushes tend to wear down your heart until it just doesn't work like it should. They fail to tell you about the meds you will have to take the rest of your life to stay alive. They need doctors teaching these courses, not old worn out officers or muscle-bound freaks. They don't tell you that your sleep will be disturbed for the rest of your lives because you have to use force on a stranger, or God forbid, you have to shoot someone. Your mind completely changes the first year of your career. You learn to trust no one. You look at everyone as the enemy. Even your own supervisors become untrustworthy strangers. The academy doesn't tell you that your spouse has no idea what you are talking about when you finally want to open up to them about your job. Oh, they do say something about divorce, but by the time that comes, the academy graduation is upon you, so you pay no attention. And then, a year or two later, your marriage is at a breaking point. Me, I'll never marry again. No one would be able to understand me now. But you know, I actually feel for anyone who works in law enforcement. It is the toughest job you will ever love. It's my greed and pride that ruined me. I guess I will never change."

You sit and just stare at Inmate Francis. You've never sat and listened to a police officer talk about their life. And now you are sitting and listening to an inmate explain their bad life choices. Here was a person who probably started out with good intentions of becoming a great officer, even became a narcotics officer, but failed to count all the costs of doing that which they knew was wrong. As you sat and stared, Inmate Francis finally said, "Are you okay? What are you looking at?" You look away and say, "You are the first law enforcement person I have ever talked to about their job. I'm amazed that anyone can take so much pressure. I'm surprised that there are any officers left on the streets. You know, I don't think anyone ever thinks about what officers go through; I know I never had before being arrested. I tell you what; my respect for the law enforcement community has changed today. Thanks for that lesson. I'm sorry for you, that it took prison for you to see the whole picture." It remained quiet for about a minute, and then Pat spoke up again. "Look, I need help, and I truly think I can trust you. How you can be happy in prison is beyond me, but I believe I want what you have. I just think I have done too much wrong. If I ever confessed all of my crimes, I promise you I would get the death penalty numerous times over. I'm going to finish out Mrs. Thomas' class because I've learned a lot, but I need you to not only pray for me, I think I need you to introduce me to your attorney. I need someone who can direct me in what or what not to say or do. My conscience has got the best of me. Is your attorney a God fearing person?" You respond, "You know what Pat, I have never asked. I know little about them. They're just handling my case. If you are trying to make amends though, I think I would start with God first. Class is only two weeks from completion. After that, I'll try and make arrangements so you can meet my attorney." You stood up, asked Pat if they were ready for chow, and the two of you along with the rest of your dorm mates, headed to the mess hall.

The rest of that week went by without another mention about your attorney, and you were glad, because you had no way of knowing how to get in touch with this person. And then, it was time for week four class with Mrs. Thomas.

Mary Thomas' face was as pretty today as you had ever seen. You had never even looked at her that way, but today her beauty radiated. And it didn't take long for her to share why. "Today," she said, "I had the privilege of leading your Warden to the Lord. This, my friends, will change the dynamics of this prison forever. You just wait and see." She beamed, not with pride, but with the glory of God. "Today's class is all about forgiveness, and I have written a scripture on the chalk board for you to not only read, but to memorize. If you get this written on your heart and on your mind, your life too, will forever change for the good." She spent more than an hour defining what forgiveness is, and what it is not. She broke it down as far as anyone could and then said, "True forgiveness is losing everything you so dearly love, and still being able to forgive the one who took your most prized possession away. That is what all of us need to survive this world; and not only survive, but to overcome it. That is what God made available at the cross. He gave His most valuable possession, His Son Jesus. And His Son gave His life so we could have a way back to our most valuable prize, a relationship with God Almighty Himself."

She looked at all of the inmates one by one and said, "You can be forgiven, no matter what you have done. Just accept what was done for you at that cross. Jesus paid the price for your sins. Life is not about what you have done; it's about what Jesus did for you. It's not based on your performance; it is based on His. God accepted His sacrifice, His blood, and that blood has covered your every sin, and mine: past, present and future. Just accept it. It's God's gift to mankind."

She gave that smile again, and your heart leaped when you looked at just how many tears were flowing from every person there, including your roommate. You let out a shout and said, "Praise God!"

What mercy she has shown towards you all these months since the death of her husband. As she goes out the door, you say, "Thank you Mrs. Thomas. Thank you for leading me to Jesus." She smiles again, and then walks back into the classroom. "Next week's class might get a little rough for some of you, but don't dare miss it. Stay out of trouble. Bye now." As pretty as she came in, she was more radiant leaving. She knew she had every inmate wanting a relationship with their creator. She had done her job and she had done it well. You could barely wait for week five class to begin.

Again you noticed how upbeat the entire prison was. It reminded you of the old prison you had come from, and how that prison had changed for the better when Mrs. Thomas arrived. You thought about the differences that had occurred in each prison; one had no disciplinary problems during class, and this class had not only lost inmates due to disciplinary infractions, but also several people lost their jobs, and several of them were arrested. Even a gun was found in class. That was scary. Your worst thought hit you when you remembered that Mrs. Thomas announced that she would no longer be presenting this class. You wondered what your future would look like as you finished out your sentence.

The rest of the week went by without incident and without your roommate inquiring about your attorney. You wondered who would show up with Mrs. Thomas for her last class, and were you ever surprised. There sat Mr. Davis with her, your attorney. You broke out in an instant sweat. You didn't think this was very wise, but Mrs. Thomas handled it like a champ. She stood to her feet and said, "Thanks for staying out of trouble and making it to the last class. As I said last week, this class might be a little rough, but I promise it will end well. Let me introduce you to a friend of mine who I found sitting in the lobby waiting to see one of his clients. The Warden had already advised him that his client was a part of this class, so I made sure to invite him in. This is Mr. Davis, and my husband and I had the privilege of introducing him to Jesus more than five years ago. He's one of my dearest friends. Introduce yourself to him after class if you need a good attorney. He doesn't mind the business and the Warden has already given his approval."

You almost fainted. You could not believe how all of this had come about. It was like someone had been listening to every conversation you and your roommate had together. And then the thought hit you; what a mighty God we serve. God was in control, and all of this was working out for the good of mankind. Even if it meant your roommate was about to be exposed. You jumped when you heard Mrs. Thomas' next words.

"You are not the victim! Do you hear me? Say it out loud! I'm not the victim. I'm the manipulator. My pity parties are over." Everything she said, she made the class repeat; and this went on for fifteen minutes, and then a hush fell over the class. Everyone watched as she walked to the chalkboard and wrote, "And I'm forgiven."

She asked if there were any questions, and your cellmate was the only person who raised their hand. She responded, "Go ahead Inmate Francis; is that right?" "Yes ma'am, that's correct. I was just wondering if you could say a prayer and maybe led us to the Lord, if you don't mind." With that, your roommate met both the Lord and your attorney that day. Pat Francis confessed their sins to God and to Mr. Davis. And with that confession, ten murders were solved within hours of Mrs. Thomas' last prison class.

Chapter Fourteen

New surroundings

Within days of the arrest of your cellmate by federal authorities, you were transferred to a prison just north of your hometown. You weren't sure if this move would be good for you, because this too was a dangerous prison. It had a reputation that competed with the first prison you were permanently assigned to. But there was a reason you were sent to this prison; as far as the prison system was concerned, you still had outstanding charges. It would actually take a court appearance to get these charges erased from your criminal records. So you sat at this prison for two months before you were finally sent out to court.

Instead of being put on a transfer bus and moved to another prison close to the courthouse, you were picked up by the county sheriff's department by court order. You had forgotten what a long ride it was down south. The officers transporting you had to make several restroom stops just for themselves. It was a miserable ride and you had not had anything to eat or drink before they had arrived. You were so glad when you got to the courthouse; and when you walked into the courtroom, there sat Mr. Davis and Ms. Smith. They approached the bench when the Judge entered into the courtroom, and all of them went into the Judge's chambers leaving you in the courtroom, with only security staff present.

After about twenty minutes, they all returned to the courtroom and the Judge asked if you would stand. You stood, still in cuffs, and listened as the Judge spoke. "I don't know what you did to impress the Governor, State and Federal authorities, and I really don't care to know. All I know is that the minimum sentence to the crimes you face here today equals a total of twenty-one years to run consecutively, and if you were found guilty, then that is the least I would give you. Inmate, I might give you all sixty years to serve. That's what you deserve. But apparently, no one wants to prosecute you anymore. If you aren't a God fearing person, then I suggest you become one. Someone is watching over you. This has never happened in my courtroom before. I suggest you don't come back."

With that, you wept all the way back to the prison, even though it was a four-hour ride, and you never once gave thought to food or water. All of your gang mess had been taken care of in one day by the courts, and you were forever grateful. You found that God's grace was sufficient and He did supply your every need.

As visitation day came around, so did your spouse and Mrs. Thomas. They sat with you all six hours, and brought you up to date on all that had been happening on the outside of those prison fences. Mrs. Thomas even shared with you her most exciting personal news she had received since her husband's death. She had moved from being interim pastor of her husband's church to being installed as senior pastor. You and your spouse were so happy for her. All of you said a prayer together for the mercy and favor God had shown upon Mary's life. What a friend that woman had become.

Before leaving, you got to hold your spouse like you should have at their father's funeral. Mrs. Thomas advised you that several other victims of incarcerated inmates were going to continue the victim impact class. You were elated to hear that. She even shared that you would be working with those inmates who had agreed to be part of this program, and that you would be moving around from prison to prison until your sentence was completed. That she said was her gift to you for doing such a good job, and of course, her favor with the Governor and the Corrections Commissioner.

She laughed; your spouse gave you a kiss, and within minutes, you were back at the dorm.

For the next several months, you got to know this prison quiet well. The Warden took a liking to you; so you got to be an aide in several classes that were being taught, and you got to see just how many vocational programs were taught at this prison. You helped out in the GED program, the adult basic education program, or ABE, and you got to audit the theological seminary program that only this prison offered in your State. Not only that, two days a week you visited the auto shop, the paint shop, the woodworking shop, and the mechanical shop. You couldn't believe the quality of work these inmates were putting out. You wondered why any inmate would ever come back to prison after learning such trades. Then it dawned on you, most inmates don't want to learn new things. They are perfectly happy right where they are in life; they hate change. You knew the simple truth of the whole matter; their irresponsibility is why they are the way they are, bottom line. You knew prison was the best place to dodge all responsibility. There, you can blame the world for victimizing you, and that's what most inmates do.

What a lesson you had learned in life. You were so thankful for God drawing you to Himself. What mercy He had given you. You looked so forward to the day you could get back to your family, and worship together with them.

Several victim impact classes came and went at this prison, and their success was as awesome as the ones you had always been involved in. Your relationship with the inmates involved forever strengthened your belief that God could change anyone who would give their life to Him.

You transferred from one prison to the other, just like Mrs. Thomas had told you; and each time a new class was completed, lives were changed. You had learned many lessons, and one of those was that all the glory belonged to God.

One day you looked up at the calendar, and low and behold, you were three months away from completing your sentence. You couldn't believe how fast the last two years had passed by. You sat down that night and wrote your spouse the most gracious letter ever. You forever thanked them for not going their own separate way. You poured out your heart to them, and all through the letter, you thanked God for saving your soul. You sealed it, stamped it, and made sure it was put in the mail. You laid your head on your pillow for the last time in this prison, because at dawn, you were awakened and told it was time to transfer again.

Chapter Fifteen

Your final transfer

You boarded the bus that morning knowing it would be your last transfer from prison to prison. You thought back at all of the people you had made acquaintance with and realized that some would remain friends forever. Before incarceration, you would have never considered even speaking to an inmate or ex-inmate, but now your view had changed for the better. These were real human beings, not just stories on the news. Every one of them had a heart, even if it was hardened. You knew from your own experience that anyone could change.

You knew when you got out of prison you had a new calling to fulfill. God had ordained you for greatness and you knew it. You knew prison ministry was a part of that calling and you were excited about your future.

You had no idea what prison you were heading to; you were just glad when the prison bus began to exit the interstate. As it reached the red light, the bus stopped. In the distance, you could see the last prison you would ever have to enter as an inmate. When the light changed, the bus pulled into the intersection and all you heard were screeching tires, and then...

The story made the front page of the local newspaper. A corrections bus was hit by an eighteen-wheeler and one inmate had lost their life. Twenty-seven other inmates and the officer driving the bus were uninjured. The driver of the truck was cited for being under the influence and arrested.

Irony has no bounds.

Chapter Sixteen

Prison's gift

As Mrs. Thomas spoke her closing words at your graveside service, she introduced Warden Harper, one of the toughest wardens in this State. As he began to speak, several inmates unloaded a headstone that they had craved in their vocational class. He said that you had been the only inmate in his thirty-year career that had made such a spiritual impact on his life and the lives of the inmates that he was responsible for. He said he wanted to do something for you and your family that would forever make others speak your name, and with that, he unveiled your tombstone. The engraved words across the top read, "Here lies a righteous and honest inmate." Below that it read in bold lettering, "THAT'S STRANGE." And at the bottom of the tombstone was written, "Connie Strange."

The Warden explained that no date was placed on the headstone because he knew you were alive in heaven.

As you looked down from heaven, you said, "The old Warden did have a sense of humor; I would have just never believed it." All heaven roared, and you went about God's business.

Conclusion

This was just a story, not true, but it could have been. None of the characters in this book are real either, nor are they similar or have a likeness to anyone I know.

Life is hard, and if anyone tells you different, then they haven't looked out their front door. The Bible says troubles will come our way. It also says to be sober, walk in soundness of mind. If you think life can't get any harder for you, then go and work in law enforcement for a season, if you're able. Something about it: it gets in your blood. Something about serving Jesus also, His blood covers you entirely.

Choices are tough sometimes, but not making a choice is a choice; and making bad choices can cost you your life. If you are a young person reading this book, then before you reject everything your parents are trying to teach you, sit down and try and count the costs of what it is you want to do. You might say, "My parents won't let me date." I say to you, "Are you ready to have a family of your own? That can happen, and does happen to thousands of young people every year. Before you ever date, let the other person know your boundaries, and stick to them. Don't ever put yourself in a situation that you can't control. Being alone with the wrong person can change your destiny forever. Guard your heart, no one else can." You say, "My parents don't like my friends." I say, "Look from their perspective and see what they see. That's a part of parenting that must be done, checking out your so-called friends. Ask yourself this. Is this someone I would go to prison for? Is this someone I would die for? I would bet not, but that also happens every day."

I know you have heard it before, but give an ear to those who have walked before you. That generation that is right ahead of you knows more than they let on. Maybe they are still living wrong, but guess what, they know what is right. Look at your parents and grandparents, if they are still alive. See if the life they have is what you want. You say, "Look here, they don't make enough money to even feed us hardly. I don't want their life. I want to make big bucks, and I want to do it fast. There's nothing wrong with selling a little weed. I need the money." I say, "Within just a few years, your parents will either be visiting you at prison, or at your graveside. If you want money, then get a real job. Get one where you don't continually have to look behind your back to see if the police are coming after you. If you want a great job, then get an education that will prepare you for your life's dreams. When your job is doing something that you love to do, then it won't seem like a job whatsoever, and you will have found your calling in this life."

Life choices: that is what they are. Are you an inmate reading this book? My prayer for you is that it humored you, at least Chapter sixteen. My prayer also is that you become able to see that hope exists only in a Savior. That Savior, Jesus Christ Himself, is waiting for you to make the one choice that will forever change your life. All the classes I mentioned in this book are real. Why don't you take the time you have left in prison and do something for yourself that is going to bring a change in your life that exceeds everything else you have ever done? That might be the one thing that keeps you from coming back to prison. That friend that is sitting next to you on the other bunk might be the very person that you hear screaming throughout eternity, if you fail to make the choice that was presented in this book. Guess what? I know the prison and jail systems let ministers in; I'm one of them. Take time and go listen to the Word of God. That's where you get faith. I know you got time, that's all you've got.

If you work in the jail or prison system and you are doing wrong, get out before you ruin another life. Don't get others injured or killed because of your greed or foolishness. Guess what, believe it or not, that happens every day of every year in the prison and jail system. Incarceration is serious business; it's not a game. Grow up! Stop the cycle of contraband and manipulation. It starts with you. Correct every wrong you see or hear about. Do what's right and do it now! Your fellow officer's lives depend on it, and so do the lives of all non-security staff members.

If you are someone who has to alter their mind with any type substance whatsoever to get through the day or to please others, please seek help; lives depend on it, even your children's. If you must for medical reasons, take drugs that alter your mindset, please don't drive. Prison is full of people, young and old, rich and poor, male and female that thought they could drive when intoxicated. Their intentions might have been good, but they are now serving time for taking a life, injuring another, or damaging property. Please don't become a statistic. There is help available throughout the world.

Now to everyone: if you think your goodness impresses God, then you are wrong. Our acceptance by God is based on Jesus' performance, not ours. Through Jesus came grace, and it freed us from the law that strengthened sin. Live in grace and accept God's mercy. Quit trying to live by the law in the Old Testament; you can't fulfill it, nor can you mix it with the New Testament. That's why it's called new. Only Jesus fulfilled the law. Thank God that He gave us His only begotten Son.

Do you want change? Just like Inmate Strange, Inmate Francis, they finally saw and realized that they could not save themselves. Someone took time to tell them about Jesus. Someone shared with them what salvation meant.

It's simple, but it will be life changing. Are you ready? Let's read together.

Matt. 4:17 ...Repent: for the kingdom of heaven is at hand. (This is Jesus speaking. He's saying, turn away from those things that aren't of God. Confess your sins and begin to live for Jesus and in Jesus. His kingdom is closer than you think.)

Romans 10:9 That if thou shalt confess with thy mouth the Lord Jesus, and shalt believe in thine heart that God hath raised Him from the dead, thou shalt be saved.

John 3:16 For God so loved the world, that He gave His only begotten Son, that whosoever believeth in Him should not perish, but have everlasting life.

You know what? You are the whosoever this verse is referring to. Receive God's gift; it's already been paid for by Jesus. You just have to believe.

Printed in the United States
By Bookmasters